A ROOM in DODGE CITY

Volume 2

The Blut Branson Era

A ROOM in DODGE CITY

Volume 2

The Blut Branson Era

A Novel-in-Vignettes

David Leo Rice

Illustrations by
Hosho McCreesh

Alternating Current Press
Boulder, Colorado

A Room in Dodge City 2: The Blut Branson Era
David Leo Rice
©2021 Alternating Current Press

Alternating Current
Boulder, Colorado
press.alternatingcurrentarts.com

ISBN: 978-1-946580-21-4
First Edition: January 2021

ADVANCE *Praise*

David Leo Rice's *Dodge City 2* is psychedelic, epistemological: it upholds and extends traditions as vital as Lynchian body horror and Barthelme-style slapstick, but its elegant and star-tling figurations are all its own. Does America contain Dodge City or vice versa? How many David Cronenbergs do we need? Rice fans out these—and other, subtler—questions with a master's hand, and delivers a book that is at once hilari-ous and profound. He's the real deal.
— Matthew Specktor, author of *American Dream Machine* and *That Summertime Sound*

Dodge City 2 is the Künstlerroman on acid, a heady investiga-tion of creation, originality, and collapse. At once a parody of and tribute to film culture, it reads like what might happen if William S. Burroughs got loaded and did a cut-up using issues of *Cahiers du Cinéma* from an alternate dimension.
— Brian Evenson, Shirley Jackson Award-winning author of *Song for the Unraveling of the World*

"Reading David Leo Rice's *Dodge City 2* is like walking through the desert on peyote, a hallucinatory dream full of surprises and gifts. It's as absurd and haunting and funny as anything I've read in a long time. Rice's baroque style and voice is fantastic. You won't be able to put it down."
— Brandon Hobson, National Book Award finalist and author of *The Removed*

"I am in a film noir affair with David Leo Rice's *A Room in Dodge City Volume 2*: I could go back to my normal life, I could embrace everything that is safe and bland and supposedly real, I could even watch a movie that bears no resemblance to any directed by Blut Branson (he of the vertiginous backstory). But why would I do that when I can have the glorious chaos, the darkly absurd humor, the mind-bending trippiness found in *The Blut Branson Era*? Maybe the banal's for you; it ain't for

me. And anyway, if I have questions, I can always ask the Official Spokesperson for What's Really Going On Here."
—Andrew Farkas, author of *The Big Red Herring*, *Sunsphere*, and *Self-Titled Debut*

"Go deep enough into certain cinematic subcultures and the term 'cult film' begins to take on an unsettling new significance. In *A Room in Dodge City Volume 2: The Blut Branson Era*, David Leo Rice ventures into the legacy of a filmmaker who may very well transcend the concept of identity itself. Add some memorably bizarre settings to the mix, plus a touch of body horror, and you have a narrative perfectly made to captivate cinephiles and devotees of the Weird in equal measure."
—Tobias Carroll, author of *Reel*, *Transitory*, and *Political Sign*, and editor of *Vol. 1 Brooklyn*

"At first *Dodge City 2* is like a Donald Barthelme script for a Coen brothers movie; then it's like a Pynchon script for a Lynch movie; then it's like a script by a writer from another universe for a director from another universe. In any case, the imaginary movie will be playing inside your head long after you finish the book. *Dodge City 2* could actually be infinite; its pages are but one dip into that other universe. This is an origin story that shirks all beginnings and all endings, serving instead an incredibly elegant assortment of crisp and cinematic scenes that add up to more than the sum of their parts. Reading it does something strange and beautiful to your experience of time. It's a fascinating, funny, disturbing, and utterly worthwhile trip."
—Elvia Wilk, author of *Oval*

"I have never in my life dreamed of a location for one of my films and failed to find it somewhere upon the Earth."
—Blut Branson,
Branson on Branson: The Master Speaks

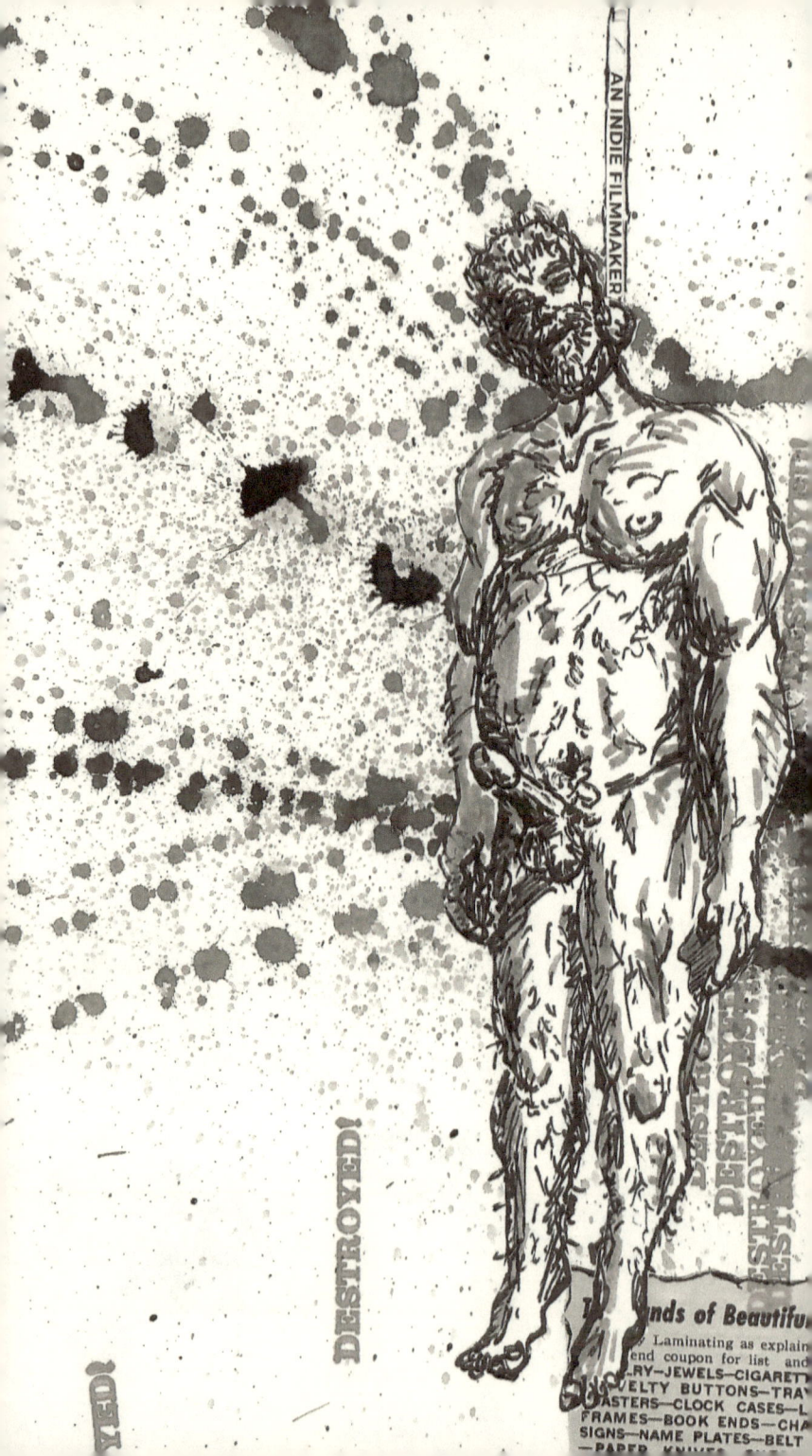

PROLOGUE 1:

The Dodge City Film Festival

IT IS SAID, by some, that during a much earlier iteration of The Dodge City Film Festival, perhaps even as far back as The Dodge City Golden Age, Blut Branson went into his room in the Hotel and hanged himself.

His film, whichever it was at that point, was playing as the Centerpiece Event that evening, but the Great Director was absent. When the lights came up in the Temple to rapturous applause and even—according to some—a standing ovation, he did not take the stage along with his producers for the Q&A.

Inevitably, an Intern was sent to the Hotel to look for him, first at the Hotel Bar, where Branson was not found, and then up to his room. After knocking seven times, it is said, the Intern convinced a maid to open the door with her skeleton key, and there the two of them found the Great Man hanging, pants around his ankles, erection pointed at the wall.

For a Director of any lower stature, this would have been the end, the cutting-short of a promising career. A tragic if not entirely unexpected outcome. But for Blut Branson, it was only the beginning. The Intern, tiptoeing out of the room in terror, was stopped in his tracks by what he later described as an un-mistakable groan coming from the corpse's direction.

He turned to look, assuming there must be someone else in the room. "Even maybe Branson's murderer, I thought," he later claimed, though the signs of Suicide were hardly subtle.

●

NO, the actual situation was far stranger. The actual situation was that Branson jiggled on his noose and hissed, "Get a note-pad, kid."

Like so, Branson directed his next film while hanging where he'd been found, using the Intern as a go-between, or Assistant Director, giving him instruction throughout the day as the poor kid ran up and down the stairs, between the room and the set, hastily assembled in the parking lot behind the Hotel, once the Festival had dispersed.

The hanging Branson would talk to no one but this Intern, so on those not-infrequent occasions when others entered the room in hopes of verifying that what the Intern said was true, it would appear that it was not. They would see nothing but a corpse, hanging there, blue-faced and veiny, its erection dwindling as days became weeks and then months.

Though no one had the guts to cut him down, there came to be those in Dodge City who claimed the Intern was a fraud, bearing False Witness for the sake of foisting his own second-rate film upon a frightened and bereft populace.

●

ONCE THIS FILM WAS FINISHED and shown at the following year's Festival, however, these same dissenters were forced to change their tune. "He's a Genius!" they began to say of the Intern, despite his refusal to accept credit. "He's the new Branson! The heir apparent, the Great Man reincarnated!" this not-insignificant part of The Dodge City Population now asserted.

"All I did was what he told me," the Intern maintained, in press conference after press conference on DCTV, until something yet stranger occurred: the press burst into the room where Branson was supposedly hanging and found no one there.

●

"HE MUST BE in another room then. . . . S-someone must have moved him," the Intern stammered, uneasy now, but no corpse was ever found, and in the years that followed, the Intern—now universally referred to as Blut Branson—directed some twenty more feature films, all smash hits at The Dodge City Film Festival, and at least twelve of them bonafide masterpieces.

There are also those who, in Dodge City's ever-bifurcating and trifurcating Oral Tradition, give the story a different ending: the Intern, this vocal minority insists, crept back into the room when the reporters and other prurient parties were distracted and affixed his own neck to the empty noose and kicked over the desk chair he'd climbed up on, quickly and gracelessly ending his own life so that, when the crowd returned, they'd find a body hanging there and, even if it could not be confirmed as Branson's—has anyone definitively seen Branson in the flesh?—it could at least be counted present, and dead, and thus put to rest. It is here, this minority claims, that the original split between the Body and the Spirit of Blut Branson came into being: the way in which he must always be considered both Living and Dead, Real and Imaginary, Present and Absent. Always both, never one or the other.

The newly dead Intern, as one subset of those who tell this story tends to put it, subsequently possessed an Intern of his own, reiterating the entire Origin Story at the next year's Film Festival, thus creating a "Branson double-prime," a stand-in's stand-in.

●

I ADMIT, hearing all of this now—up in my Room with Big Pharmakos, just down the hall from where the story takes place—that I identify most with the Intern. I put myself in his role, almost as if I'm playing him in the Movie of the story I've just been told, with Blut either playing himself or being played by a convincing Impersonator, a situation that, though I don't know it yet, will end up defining the coming period of my life in Dodge City, in which I'll try, again and again and again, to find my way to the Real Blut Branson, only to discover that the ranks of Impersonators are extremely deep, likely infinite, so that between me, where I stand now, creeping past the beginning of my life and into its presumptive middle, and Branson himself, the Great Man in all his glory, is perhaps nothing but a vast quantity of fiction.

PROLOGUE 2:

Purge of the Impersonators

SOMETIME AFTER BIG PHARMAKOS' STORY ENDS, and he leaves me alone in my Room, I look out the window to see a bonfire crackling in the center of Sacrifice Square. Though I don't yet know if I'll end up running toward or away from it, I put on my shoes and coat and head downstairs through the Lobby, and outside to where a crowd has gathered.

I see Big Pharmakos and hurry toward him.

"They're purging the films of the Impersonators," he explains, without my having to ask. He knows me well by now, I think, not without pride. "Any films not attributable to Branson go on the pyre. Every year, it's gotta be done. Otherwise, they just keep piling up. Films like these get made whether or not anyone wants them to. Pretty soon, if we weren't careful, Branson would be just one Director among many!"

As he speaks, a dump truck unloads a fresh pile of DVDs and videocassettes, even though, as Big Pharmakos explains, "Branson's films only exist on celluloid and are only ever shown at the Temple. No home-viewing for the Holiest of Holies, except on pirated tapes." His tone drops to a whisper, somewhere between pious and resentful. It's hard to tell through all the smoke.

"All my stand-up specials are in there," he laments, wiping his eyes as the pyre grows. The people of Dodge City strip to their underwear and dance barefoot around it, arms outstretched, chanting, "Blut! Blut! There is no God but God! God is good and God is God and there is no Blut but God and no God but Blut!"

"Do they ever burn a Blut film by accident?" I whisper.

Big Pharmakos smacks me across the mouth and leans in to snarl, "Don't ever ask anything like that again!"

I can't tell if he shares my skepticism and is warning me about the danger posed by others, or if he's as devout as the dancing masses, though the fact that he's still standing beside me, rather than joining in, would seem to imply that . . .

Now I'm dancing, too, despite the throbbing in my jaw. We both are. "Burn! Burn!" we shout. "Burn, heretics, burn!"

The fire crackles and spits so loudly it sounds like we're burning the actual heretic filmmakers, not just their films . . . and now, suddenly, I can't be sure we're not. The air fills with blood and sweat, and I want to vomit, but the adrenaline won't let me. So, I run and chant, bodies slamming into me whenever I stop, ash from the fire leaping out to singe my toes.

"No God but Blut, no films but Blut's!" We chant it again and again, until the air gets so smoky it either goes black or I black out. In the blackness, I feel all memory of my early work leaching away, melting into the same Pit of Souls to which I've always imagined human consciousness reverting after Death. Whatever films I've made up to this point, whatever scripts I've written, if any, if my Life in Movies were ever more than idle aspiration, are lost to me now. When I come-to, I'll be a blank slate, a man in his thirties as new to the world as he was at five—a null set, a neophyte, a mental infant with joints already beginning to stiffen.

●

I COME-TO on my knees in front of a movie theater with a marquee sign that reads THE TEMPLE over the entrance, and a set of twenty-seven marble stairs leading up to its double-doors.

I'm still on my knees, where, apparently, I've been long enough to count all the stairs. I feel myself moving toward them, one knee-length at a time, the crowd sluggishly approaching as those who've reached the top make their way inside.

When my turn comes, I shuffle along with Big Pharmakos, trying to keep my head up despite the tears the smoke forces me to cry. I try to remember my name—the one Dalton gave me in Sacrifice Square, once it became clear that I wouldn't be leaving Dodge City—but find that I can't. That, too, seems to have been purged in the smoke. So much for being someone, I think, not without a modicum of relief.

"Pray," Big Pharmakos whispers, and I look over and see his lips puttering, though I can't tell if they're emitting sound. Either way, I putter along.

●

FINALLY, we make it to the top of the stairs and crawl over the threshold into the Temple, past the mobbed concession stand and the walls covered with movie posters. *The Pale Oaks: A Blut Branson Film* and *The Murder of Nicola Teensmah: A Blut Branson Film* catch my eye.

Past the Lobby, done up in a mixture of Aztec and Egyptian styles, we enter the main theater, which smells of ancient, sanctified popcorn and rancid butter. And of darker things, too: blood, urine, semen, sweat. The kind of theater I've heard of, in Old Times Square or certain stretches of West Hollywood, or Amsterdam maybe, South Beach, the Castro, Istanbul, the Pigalle in Paris . . . but those are all just words to me, whereas the smells and the atmosphere in here are rich and immediate—the crackling possibility of getting stabbed in the dark, the tantalizing, somewhat shameful awareness that, should something onscreen awaken in me the urge to touch myself, no one in the surrounding dark would look askance on my following that urge through to fruition.

Instead, blasphemous as it sounds to admit, the pyre and the dancing and the knee-crawling have so exhausted me that I fall asleep as soon as the main feature begins. I dream of an angry usher shaking me awake and demanding an explanation for my lapse in focus, to which I reply, "It was simply so holy I couldn't bear to watch."

●

WHEN I WAKE UP, I'm holding a ticket that says, "Admit One to Dinner at Branson Mansion," and Big Pharmakos is leading me out of the theater saying, "Welcome to Dodge City in earnest, my friend."

PROLOGUE 3:

Dinner at Branson Mansion

UNFOLDING THE TICKET, I read it more closely in the light of the smoldering pyre outside:

"MR. BRANSON (or his surrogate) HAS DE-CIDED TO OFFER YOU THE PLEASURE OF HIS COM-PANY THIS EVENING, AT HIS HOME, WITH HIS WIFE (or companion). A CAR WILL BE WAITING FOR YOU IN FRONT OF THE TEMPLE."

I crumple it just as the car—a black limo—pulls up to where I'm standing. I get in and watch as the windows are milked over, and we pull onto what I can only imagine is a private-access road leading out of Town, through the foothills of a mountain range I'd never known was there.

When I give up trying to make out shapes through the windows, I let myself slip into a fantasy of being driven up Mulholland Drive, out of the basin of L.A. and into the mountains, where the true shadowy power players live. I've imagined it often enough, sculpting a dream-topography of L.A. out of whatever notional setting I happened to find myself in, dreaming of a Life in Movies, a steady Westward Expansion that has, at long last, brought me here.

Now that it's really happening, I'm overwhelmed. I close my eyes and pretend I'm back in my Room, still waiting for something to happen.

●

THE DRIVER STOPS and points toward a cobbled path lit by electric torches recessed in rosebushes, winding along a steep ridge, too narrow to drive on, toward what appears to be a mansion overlooking the ocean.

Before I can think of anything to ask—no specific question comes to mind, though I feel insufficiently informed in a general sense—he's gone. So, I follow the path, from torch to torch, along the clifftop, listening to the sound of the ocean, which I know almost for certain is nowhere near Dodge City, and yet there it is, so either I'm dreaming or the world isn't how I've always pictured it, or both.

All that matters is that I'm knocking on a door, waiting, and then being let in by an attractive woman of unplaceable origin, about my age if not younger.

"Come in, come in," she says, and leaves me to close the door, take my shoes off—hers are off, so I figure mine should be, too —and follow her down the hall, past a fireplace, a sleeping dog, a room piled with books and magazines, and into a kitchen where a middle-aged man sits icing his knee, foot up on the chair across from him.

●

AFTER AN APERITIF of Campari Sodas and chili peanuts, we sit at the dinner table passing around plates of shredded turkey, carrot salad, and roasted potatoes. Conversation is hushed when it isn't nonexistent.

I look from Branson to his wife—if these are indeed their roles —and back again, wondering if they'll ever ask me about myself or broach the reason I was invited here. If they don't by the time I've finished what's on my plate, I decide, I'll ask them.

"So, Mr. Branson," I begin, when I've finished what was on my plate. "Can I ask what you're working on? Any big projects underway?"

"Working on?" his wife—if she is his wife—asks, while Branson continues to eat like he plays no part in this exchange.

"I mean," beginning to mince words now, not quite sure what I'm getting myself into, "like any new films or anything?"

"Films?" She looks at me like I'm asking if she can see the UFO I've just claimed is hovering outside the window.

I start to sweat. Am I in the right house? I wonder, my worries starting slow and concrete before ramping up and spinning out. Did I get lost along the path? Did the driver drop me off at the wrong address?

As no verified images of Blut Branson exist, it's impossible to say what he looks like. The middle-aged man icing his knee across the table could be anyone.

The couple chews and looks me over, and I fear they're reading my mind. In case they are, I force myself to think positively —dogmatically—about the Great Man. Yes, I think. Branson is real. Branson is great. He is . . . but what if he's . . .? I mean, who's to say that he's not, in fact, actually a . . .?

Now I'm trying to force myself to stop thinking. My head still feels thick from the smoke in Sacrifice Square. "I just meant," I say, hoping to reintegrate myself, "since Blut Branson's the most renowned Director in the history of Dodge City, um . . . I was just wondering if he was, you know . . . if you were . . . working on anything new?"

She looks at me with concern, as her husband, or whoever he is, takes more turkey and smacks his lips. "Who's Blut Branson?" she asks, like I haven't just told her. Her English is confident, but her accent—Hungarian, Turkish, Maltese, Swiss?— is thick.

"The most renowned Director in the history of . . ." I speak slowly. So slowly, it turns out, that I forget what I was trying to say before I finish saying it. When I've caught my breath, I change tack and ask, "Your husband . . . what's his name?"

Both of them stare at me, chewing without swallowing.

"Look, we invited you here because we thought it would be fun to meet someone new, and fun for you, as well, but if you're going to interrogate us in our own home . . . we're going to, well . . . you can just go right back where you came from and stay there."

She finally swallows and gets up from the table, taking her plate with her. "C'mon, honey," she says, "help me in the kitchen." The man takes a big gulp from his wineglass and follows her, limping as he carries his plate, leaving me alone with mine.

●

I SIT AT THE TABLE, wondering if they're ever coming back. For a while, I can hear them in the kitchen, washing dishes and talking indistinctly.

Then I can't anymore. I can't tell if they've retreated to another room—bed, perhaps—or left the house, or if they were figments all along.

In the silence, I think, Perhaps this is my house. Perhaps it has been all along, and I'm only now remembering, or perhaps it isn't yet but will be soon. Yeah, I think, that's it. This is all a premonition, a sign that, soon enough, I'll be Blut Branson, and his mansion, overlooking the ocean off the coast of L.A., high in the hills over Mulholland Drive, will be mine.

I'm ebullient now, drinking wine from the half-empty bottles left out on the table, my heart pounding, ambition and adrenaline surging through me, making my neck and armpits steam.

●

I GET UP and wander among the rooms, imagining I've lived here alone for decades, plotting my masterpieces, preparing to unleash them on the brute, adoring masses in the valley below.

Maybe there's no problem, I think. You're just at home, having an off-night. No big deal. I wander through the study, the map room, the home cinema, and then upstairs, in search of the Master Bedroom.

On the upper landing, my skin crawls. I have enough sanity— or stubbornness—left to reject the fantasy before it consumes me, and to remember that I'm alone in a strange house, one that I'm not sure I want to be welcomed any deeper into, even if the invitation still stands.

●

So, I hurry back downstairs, past the couple now standing in the kitchen doorway, holding dishrags and staring at me, and outside, back along the nerve-racking clifftop path to the driveway where the limo dropped me off.

I find it still idling where it was, unless it left and has just returned. Though no one's chasing me, I heave the door open and dive in sideways across the backseat, shouting, "Drive! Drive! Drive!" The driver does, calm as a stuntman in a heist film.

I sit up and catch my breath as we wind down from the hills. When I can speak in my normal tone again, I say, "Sorry about that. I just had to pop in to check on something. Didn't think I'd be so long."

The driver responds by turning on the radio, which blares static pocked by two voices, one male, the other female. Though I can't be sure, I sense that it's the couple from the mansion, sending me a message, or a warning, as I return to Dodge City.

I close my eyes and let myself slip—at first a little at a time, and then all the way, a plummet—back into the fantasy of being Blut Branson, on my way to work in my private car, heading out to the Desert where my sets are dressed and ready to go, the cast and crew and all the extras awaiting my arrival in reverent silence.

Soon, I think, my Movie will be finished and then all of Dodge City will exist solely in the realm of my fantasy. My dreams, I think, Branson's voice loud inside my skull, will become their reality, and all will at last be as it should.

●

DO NOT GUARD

PHASE I:

Unholy Family

(Watching TV)

Before the Law

RESENSITIZED TO THE FACT that I have no firm grip on what's really afoot here, I let the Branson-reverie wear off as I sink back into being me, alone in my Room, far from any Life in Movies.

Turning on the TV, I decide, for the time being, simply to take things as they come. Unlike Movies, TV strikes me as a Director-less medium, an endless undifferentiated stream of data, shaped by no particular vision and manifesting the tyrannical dictates of no singular Will. A holy, or unholy, ghost, adrift in a universe without a God.

Nevertheless, there are those who claim that Blut Branson isn't merely in reclusion, but rather, that he's transformed into a TV Director. "Movies are on the out; TV's on the in" is a phrase that's started making the rounds during the leadup to the new season of *Unholy Family*. "Unlike Dodge City itself, TV's in a Golden Age," I hear more than one talking head declare. "So, if Blut wants to guest-direct an *Unholy Family* season, who's to say he shouldn't?"

I shrug, though, in my heart, I know the answer.

●

STILL, halfway hoping to encounter Blut in the process, I venture out of my Room and through the side streets to the office complex where *Unholy Family* is allegedly produced, deep in the bowels of DCTV, located behind the train tracks, just across the Strip, on the near side of The Dodge City Annex. The new season hasn't started yet—we're still in the thick of reruns—so I figure now's as good a time as any to get my foot in the door.

I go with my résumé every day for a week but never make it past the Waiting Room. Like the inner sanctums of the Law in Kafka's *Before the Law*, which I've just reread to be sure the comparison is apt, I remain totally cut off from the behind-the-scenes world of *Unholy Family*. My pleas of "Isn't there someone I can talk to?" fall on deaf ears, though one time an Intern tells me, "Don't you know *Unholy Family*'s a reality show? Why would you apply to work for them when you're working for them already, just by being here, alive in Dodge City?"

Then, as I've come to expect by now, I'm shown the door. Needless to say, I discover no sign of Blut, which affirms my suspicion that he'd never sully himself by working in TV. No, I think, leaving DCTV for the last time, Blut Branson is still out there, high in the hills, dreaming, plotting, planning his Return to Movies.

A Run-In with Drifter Jim

SHAKEN FROM THIS WEEK of futile striving, I walk toward the Outskirts to clear my head. Though the air out here is toxic—filled with pesticide runoff, fumes from the refinery, and hog feces the farmers spray into the air—it feels good to get away from the center.

I walk up the Strip, past the mostly empty big-box stores, the methadone clinic, and the bail bonds office. I want to walk as far as I can before reaching the point at which I'll have to decide whether to cross into the Desert.

I think about my tenure here in Dodge City, about whether to move on yet again, which I've repeatedly decided not to do, on the logic that no place will offer more or less than this one does—that the battle is largely, if not entirely, internal—so I once again decide to stick it out, though not without worrying that Dodge City is thinking through me, forcing me to this conclusion against my Will. But what would my Will, if unfettered, prefer? What, if any, are the opportunities I'm not pursuing?

●

STYMIED, as I always am after any serious attempt to think, I stop into the first gas station convenience store I see, situated right at the edge of the Desert. "The Last Gas Station & Gas Station Convenience Store," reads a banner hanging over its door, which dings as I open it.

Inside, the air smells of broken air-conditioning and cat litter. I suck it in, too tired to hold my breath, and rummage in the frostbitten back cooler for a can of Cherry Coke. Bringing it to the register, I look up from the rack of crumpled smut magazines and Snus, to see a familiar face manning the till.

"Drifter Jim?" I ask. I haven't seen or heard any mention of him since meeting him on my very first night in the Hotel.

He doesn't exactly blush, but something like shame comes over his face, in the shadow of its massive cowboy hat, as he nods.

"I thought you'd left Town years ago. Didn't you go to Denver?"

He rings up my Cherry Coke and scowls, making me regret having asked. "Sometimes we just get as far as we can," he says, taking my two dollars without giving me change.

I nod, aware, in a sense, of what he means. "Well, good seeing you," I mumble, cracking open the can and taking a swig. It tastes off, like dirty ice has seeped through the metal, but I don't say anything. "Good luck," I say, on my way out.

"Want a word to the wise?" Drifter Jim asks, adjusting his cowboy hat and flicking at one of the lighters from the rack on the counter. "Stay in your Room. Turn on the TV and chill. You're not missing anything out here."

"The Dodge City

Partial-Abortion Scheme":

Unholy Family Season Premiere

TAKING **DRIFTER JIM'S ADVICE** without asking myself whether it was friendly or threatening, I finish my Cherry Coke in the relative comfort of my Room, TV blaring on high.

The BREAKING NEWS, though it comes as no surprise after my visit to DCTV, is that *Unholy Family* has officially become a reality show. "This season, news and entertainment are finally one!" a banner proclaims at the bottom of the screen. "At last: one sacred, indivisible whole! All of us here in Dodge City are part of a single, tremendous Unholy Family, and never again will this fact be obscured behind a veneer of fiction! No Director can hide the truth any longer! There is no art. There is no life. There is only the *Unholy Family Season Premiere*!"

The screen shows a preview of the *Season Premiere*, in which numerous familiar faces congregate around a tank in Sacrifice Square, but now the question of whether they're actors reprising their old roles, or Dodge City citizens caught in the act of living here, is hard to answer. My own face, reflected in the glass of the screen, seems, at the same time, to be coming from within the shot, so that it grows hard to say whether I'm sitting here, in my Room, or standing there, beside the tank, staring into a camera.

●

AS I WAIT for this disturbance to normalize, the preview becomes the real thing. The *Season Premiere* centers on The Dodge City Annual Abortion Rally, in which each side, pro and con, repeats its position from last year, competing to get as close to verbatim as possible. Though I still see myself in the crowd, I no longer consider this unusual.

"It's a simple matter of matching fetus to tube," Professor Dalton, reprising his role of Chief Epistemologist, begins. "A one-to-one correspondence in which nothing is wasted. I could do the procedure myself. Right here, right now. If you would only let me."

Big Pharmakos, on a Conservative tear after a recent onstage meltdown stalled his rise to the top of comedy, holds the mantle for the opposition. "Fuck them for not wanting to be born! I didn't want to be born, either, but here I am! Right?! Aren't we all here? Well . . . aren't we?!"

A moment later, he adds, "It's a serious question. Are we, or aren't we?"

Each voice magnifies another until it blends into a single Town-sized shriek that rattles the speakers on my TV. Soon men, women, babies, and *Unholy Family* crewmembers are fighting openly, tearing at one another's clothes, spitting in one another's faces, and elbowing one another in the ribs.

●

THIS IMPASSE IS FINALLY BROKEN by the arrival of a pilgrim dragging a tank on a cart. After a crewmember runs over to ask, the name Blanche Brine Daly is displayed across the bottom of the screen.

"My tank," Blanche begins, with no sequiter, as the crowd-noise sinks beneath that of her voice, "is meant for those fetuses that are not yet ready to be born, or those mothers that are not yet ready to bear them. The interior conditions mimic the life-sustaining conditions of the womb, but not the life-*developing* conditions, so that the fetus can survive *as is*, without being transformed against its Will—or its mother's—into a baby."

A pause while we subject her tank to scrutiny, reprising the image from the preview shown earlier.

"So, there is no net loss of life. Nor any net gain. No, sirs. I offer only the chance to . . . arrest development until the time is right. Until solid groundwork can be laid. A genuine compromise to bring an end to all this madness."

Looking out at the bloodied citizenry gathered before her, she eases the tank off the cart and settles it onto the ground. "It's an open-air device," she begins. "As fine a piece of kit as you're likely to find anyplace this side of Chicago, where far finer are to be found. But if anyone were the Chicago-type, they wouldn't be here today. Am I right?" Her question sounds genuine, not rhetorical, but elicits only murmurs.

"Does anyone have an extension cord?" she asks, apparently willing to let her first question go unanswered, and it's a long time before we realize she's still talking to us. When we do, we have to ask her to repeat the question, which she does, but it turns out that none of us has one, so we all have to entertain ourselves while she goes to the hardware store during a commercial break.

The *Unholy Family* crew shoots B-reel and eats trail mix until she returns with the extension cord, seemingly attached to a power source inside the Bar, and plugs in the tank, bringing its brine to life.

●

"**WELL**, step right up, ladies. Don't be shy," she says, after we've all stood dumbfounded for as long as she'll let us. "Any woman will do."

Finally, a woman none of us knows steps forward and waits beside the tank while Blanche looks her over. "Any *pregnant* woman," Blanche clarifies.

The woman pauses, like she's trying to remember what she'd meant to say, then says, "I could get pregnant."

Blanche looks her over again, shaking her head. "No time for that now. This is a live demonstration."

Looking cornered, the woman faints or pretends to faint on the concrete, and another woman, fantastically pregnant, steps over her.

Blanche looks satisfied. She blindfolds this woman, spins her three times, and proceeds to extract the fetus using nothing but her thumb and index finger, each of which has been outfitted—we see this in closeup—with an extra joint in the middle.

This woman falls on top of the other. "Now, two non-pregnant women are collapsed in a pile for different reasons," the *Unholy Family* announcer informs us.

The fetus, meanwhile, is already in the tank, where it hovers before burrowing into a sediment on the bottom, stirring it up, clouding our view.

"It is planted in a sediment that will not permit it to grow," says Blanche, removing her extra finger joints, wiping them on a handkerchief, and putting them back in their carrying case. "When the mother is ready, be that days or years from now, the fetus will be reimplanted and carried to term, as if there'd been no interruption at all."

●

UNHOLY FAMILY ELIDES many subsequent iterations of the process, picking back up when the tank is full of fetuses, ranging from a few weeks to nearly nine months of age. The tank is so full that some of its brine has bubbled over the edges, frothing on the concrete below, eating into it.

In the next cut, all the mothers are in a giant heap at the edge of the liquid's reach, breathing as one. "Now," says Blanche, "I feel about as tired as they look. I presume that is a Hotel over there?"

●

LIKE SO, she becomes a temporary part of Dodge City, in a room just down the hall from mine, perhaps the very same one where Blut or Blut's proxy either did or did not hang himself at The Dodge City Film Festival, long ago.

Days later, when *Unholy Family* asks her what happens now, all she says is, "I've sent for my husband from Chicago. He should be here any day."

The mothers continue to lie beside the tank, unmoving, blanketed in the shadows of their fetuses. Big Pharmakos fashions a rough wooden paddle and takes it upon himself to stir the brine, but when the *Unholy Family* crew asks him to "stop tampering with the evidence," he proves surprisingly compliant, returning to the Hotel's Function Room to rehearse his now-suspect comedy routine.

Unholy Family puts a "Do Not Guard" sign around the tank, to ensure that nothing comes between it and whatever's going to happen. Life stays normal for longer than feels normal.

I perch in my window and look out at the wind rippling the brine, sometimes bringing the fetuses' half-formed faces to the surface. I name the ones with defined features and try to keep track of them until they sink back under.

●

AFTER A WEEK, Blanche reports that her husband arrived several days ago and that "we've been living in marital bliss ever since," but the *Unholy Family* crew is unable to find any evidence of him.

In between updates, rumors circulate that a marauder is loose in the surrounding woods, picking off chickens and making fetishes from their bones, but we assume these are mostly intended to dilute our attention, so we try not to let them.

Which is a shame, because if we'd been more attuned to this side of the story, some of us might have seen the thing steal in from the woods last night, covered in pine needles and chicken blood, and climb into the tank, sloshing more brine over the edge, partially dissolving the dormant mothers.

When we wake and head down to Sacrifice Square the next morning, we see something slipping around with the fetuses, swirling them together, seeping into their thin shells, squeezing sound from those that have lungs. The whole tank has a gamey reek now, like a jar of pickles left open in a dead fridge.

Blanche is there, too, in her bathrobe, her gaze serene as the fetuses start to grow. Whether they're three-week specks or eight-month behemoths, they swell up, reaching and surpassing the size of human babies, taking on shapes that borrow from the human template without respecting it. Many of them look vegetal, with cabbage-like flaps and turnip hair.

Their bodies turn thick and spongy, their sourdough faces pressed against the glass. Soon, all the brine has been forced out onto the mothers, whose bodies are mostly dissolved, and the fetuses are huge creatures standing mushed together inside the tank, groaning, trying to chew through the glass with lips that contain only more lips.

The marauder is nowhere to be seen: its body has been absorbed, spent in the process of making them what they are now. In this moment, we forget that they once had human fathers—many of whom are standing right here, in the crowd—and accept that whatever came into the tank last night is their True Father now.

"It's as if," says Dalton, all too happy to resume his position of authority, "they were nothing but unfertilized eggs all this time, and now, at last, after months in the incubator, some sperm has come to fertilize them. Think about the implications. . . . Imagine that you and I, right now, are likewise unfertilized, waiting for our True Father to find us and make us into what we will one day be . . . and all along we've thought of ourselves as full creatures already."

He goes on, but Blanche interrupts him. "Excuse me, folks, but does anyone have a hammer? I really ought to let these fellows out."

Again, no one answers, so, again, she goes to the hardware store to buy one, or to take one, since the hardware store owner is out here with us.

After she's smashed the tank, we watch as the doughy creatures stomp off, some on feet and some not, grinding the bones of their mothers into the pavement, and scraping the remnants of their True Father's ejaculate from their legs and torsos.

They reach the edge of Sacrifice Square and wait, watching us. *Unholy Family* swarms around Blanche, cameras upon cameras, beyond the edge of our field of vision.

The head reporter puts the mic in her face. "So, before we try to interview these . . . things, tell us what we all want to know: is the marauder that came in from the woods last night your husband from Chicago? It is, isn't it? Just admit it! It's their father, and you're their mother, right? Right?!"

The screen fades to black on a banner that reads: "FIND OUT NEXT TIME ON *UNHOLY FAMILY*, DODGE CITY'S LONGEST-RUNNING REALITY-TV SHOW."

The Unholy Family Reunion

THE NEXT EPISODE promises an even deeper exposé of Dodge City's breeding patterns, offering "a nose-dive into the newly relevant question of where people actually come from." Needless to say, we all tune in. I'm in my Room, unsure if I've been here all along, or if I'm just getting back.

This episode, which pitches itself as a corrective to the previous one, a redrawing of Dodge City's fraught lines of heredity, though it provides no concrete answers to the questions posed before, features a group of eight at a family reunion, each of whom is introduced by way of a quick montage. Sitting around the table nursing tumblers of scotch with their napkins piled on dirty plates are Shep, a grandpa whose wife has died and left him with terminal esophageal cancer; Carlene, a single mother with a skyrocketing investment firm; her newborn, Milo, who has one hand of all thumbs and no other hand; that baby's Rilke-critic older sister, Rita; a forty-two-year-old test pilot named Marx with a sense of taste that only kicks in an hour after contact with food; Marx's wife, Sue, who has swallowed enough Percocet to end things within the hour; Sue's son from another marriage, Devon, a world-class juggler; and Devon's college roommate, Sterns, who intends to study botany if his self-service app doesn't take off, though all signs indicate that it will.

The conceit of the episode is that, now that the meal has been eaten and all the graces and toasts have been said and thanks duly given, each family member will draw a symbol on an index card representing who they currently are, and then put these cards into the hands of the *Unholy Family* host, who will shuffle and hold them back out to the family members, who will each choose one in turn.

Whichever symbol each person chooses determines who that person will be for the coming year, no questions asked. For example, if Shep, the grandpa with terminal esophageal cancer, chooses the symbol of Rita, the Rilke critic, he gets to be her for the rest of the year, no more impending doom, no more dead wife, just long, slow days alone with the poems. And if Rita, the former Rilke critic, chooses the symbol of the new-born with only one hand, then that's who she is, starting her clock back almost at zero, freeing up the newborn (assuming he's able to pick a card at all) to pick the card of, say, Sterns, the college botanist and possible app-phenom. As for Sterns, well . . .

"Anyway, that's how it works," interjects the host.

Soon, all the cards have been chosen. Almost everyone is someone else. Marx, the test-pilot, chose the card of his Perco-cet-swallowing wife and died, while his wife became Carlene, the ultra-rich single mother, and left with one of the college boys, who'd luckily chosen his own card.

●

I FIND THIS all moderately diverting as I sit on the foot of my bed sawing at a Room Service steak, but it's not what rivets me. What rivets me is an inconsistency in the numbers. All the characters remain onscreen, all eight as they accept their lots for the year to come, but there's someone else behind them, a kind of fleshed shadow.

A spotlight reveals her to be a woman in her late forties with a shaved head just starting to show stubble. I can't place her. Maybe I've never seen her before, or else she's always been in the background of *Unholy Family*, emerging from the overlap of the named characters, there but not there, like someone I've always seen around Town without once stopping to meet.

When the eight main characters are led away, this woman re-mains, staring at me from the screen. The camera lingers on her leaning against the wall of the kitchen, while the staff clears the bones and gravy from the table.

I am left with the sense that this is the essence of how the peo-ple of Dodge City reproduce: the extras who emerge from this reshuffling of family roles are the only new souls among us, and thank God for that, I think, though my actual feeling is closer to horror. Otherwise, the people of Dodge City would be a long-extinct race, and I'd be, at best, alone in a Ghost Town.

Whether this is meant to be taken as an argument against the Partial-Abortion Scheme—claiming that now more than ever our numbers must increase—or as an apologia for it—claiming that, even with the Scheme in place, the people of Dodge City will find ample means of reproducing—is hard to say, but the fact that this may be the reason why there are so many people here, especially the shadowy ones, I find impossible to refute. Looking back at the screen, I see the woman with the shaved head nod and vanish.

BREAKING NEWS:

The Death of David Cronenberg

THE *UNHOLY FAMILY* SEASON IS INTERRUPTED (or re-imagined) late Wednesday night by a blood-red streak of BREAKING NEWS: David Cronenberg has been deemed "unsustainably long in the tooth, a seven-point-five on the ten-point scale of obsolescence," after a two-year covert investigation by The Dodge City Department of Fish & Wildlife, and is thus to be consigned to an honorary plot in the Suicide Cemetery, "a nice, leafy corner for Career Suicides, those whose spirits have been aborted by their still-living bodies," according to Dalton, who now appears to be narrating the report from inside the *Unholy Family* studio.

A full survey of his works by a "panel top-heavy with experts," Dalton continues, has determined that the drop-off in filmic vitality between early-to-middle works, such as *Videodrome*, *Dead Ringers*, and *Naked Lunch*, and middle-to-late ones, such as *A Dangerous Method*, *Cosmopolis*, and *Maps to the Stars*, is regrettably sharp enough to strip him of his National Hero status, which is not, the report takes pains to remind us, a matter of opinion but rather one of policy, enshrined in the Town Charter. Simply put, "David Cronenberg is to the so-called outside world what Blut Branson is to Dodge City: the Supreme Cinematic Godhead from which our Collective Dream-life issues. The mountain spring from which the small trickle of inner life we are capable of sustaining gushes forth. That the letters *D.C.* stand for both Dodge City and David Cronenberg is lost on no one."

It is said by some, I've learned, that the people of Dodge City conceive of the nation in a fractal pattern, whereby every Town has a Blut Branson who's a model of David Cronenberg, who himself may or may not exist: he's merely the template that all local cinematic figureheads must follow. Here, as perhaps in all things, Dodge City is both smaller and larger than the nation. Branson is an avatar of Cronenberg, but, as this correspondence was itself concocted within The Dodge City Film Industry, it's equally true or indeed truer to say that Cronenberg is an avatar of Branson, just as God is said by some to be an avatar of Man, rather than vice versa.

●

I'D LIKE TO CONSIDER my knowledge of Cronenberg's filmography relatively sophisticated, but it's nothing compared to that of the people of Dodge City. To put it lightly, the full depth of what he means to them is, like so much around here, more than I can grasp.

"It's a matter of psychic security," Dalton adds, wearing what appears to be a newly tailored suit, accommodating the pounds he's put on in his semi-retirement, "since surely you'll agree that a community that maintains its Heroes past their prime is not one long for the first world. I cannot, in good faith, allow the people of this Town to continue to drink tainted water, if you'll pardon the metaphor. Sad as it is to say, we all deserve better."

'Nam-style footage of burning Cronenberg effigies being paraded by gloved hands through the streets, and of self-immolating Cronenberg Impersonators in Sacrifice Square, floods the screen.

"And," Dalton continues, "lest anyone believe this tragedy is unique to Dodge City, let me assure you all it is not. FEMA and the National Guard have been deployed at strategic locations around the country, to quiet unrest and to force a certain amount of solace on the larger population as we go through the several stages of Collective Grief."

●

I DOZE OFF HERE. When I come-to, Dalton is ordering a Work Crew to take down the thirty-foot Cronenberg effigy in Sacrifice Square, which until now had been the tallest structure visible from my window.

I hurry outside to watch in person. By the time I get out there, naked children are circling around it, crying and ripping out their hair as the Work Crew tears it from its foundation. Somewhere in the process, its head cracks off, and a hundred keening widows bear it away to a shrine in the hills, kissing its plaster lips as they roll it through the mud.

"Now, for the burial," says Dalton, taking the stage under his familiar beaked Sacrifice mask. "This, here, is both a representation of Cronenberg and the man himself," he points to the headless effigy. "Do you understand? This massive object is both the genuine D.C. and a flimsy, even blasphemous approximation thereof. Always both, never one or the other. The last terrestrial carapace of the Genius Formerly Known as David Cronenberg, as well as a mere tribute, little more than a toy, as the human body itself always ultimately is, the Soul being free as soon as," here he lights the effigy on fire, "the confines of its mortal form are shorn away by the scythe of time."

We bow our heads as the effigy turns to ash, dripping into the same pit in which we burned the last of Harry Crews a few years back. This feels, very clearly, like a retread of that, all things, it occurs to me again, being cyclical in Dodge City.

In the thick, heady smoke, I have the following thought: if Cronenberg represents what Blut Branson might have become had he left Dodge City and taken his chances in the wider world, then his death—be it symbolic or literal—releases his spirit back into the ether. Perhaps it's now up for grabs, floating free, in search of a new host.

Could that host be me? I want to speculate further but can tell the crowd is about to turn feral, so I make a mental note to revisit this question later.

Pageant of the New Cronenberg

ERE, FEMA steps in. It kicks Dalton off the stage and shoots a fire hose at the smoldering effigy in the pit, though it's too late to salvage anything but ash. When the smoke clears, FEMA explains that a Pageant is to be held.

"Due to technicalities arising from the fact that Cronenberg is what is known in German as a *Grenzgänger*, or border-walker, being at once a Canadian citizen and an American icon, the task of replacing him is not as straightforward as the layman might expect."

FEMA takes a moment here to compose itself, apparently surprised at how emotional this is all becoming. It continues, "So, rather than appointing a replacement on the national level, behind closed doors, we are leaving it to you, the people. The Cronenberg-spirit, loosed from its former housing, is now at large, free to settle and reassert itself where it will. Mothers, fathers, abductors . . . anyone with access to promising young folk, we urge you to enter your little boy or girl into the running. Out of all the applicants, one New Cronenberg will be chosen. All applicants must be under twenty, to ensure a maximally long and fruitful career. The first round of judging will be held in Sacrifice Square one week from today. Now get busy!" FEMA shoots its .45 in the air, and everyone scatters.

●

OVER THE COURSE of this week, I roam Dodge City, intrigued to see the rehearsals underway. Parents with kids aged five to eleven occupy all available space, taking over stores and restaurants, the capacious interior of the Dead Mall, and all the sidewalks and sometimes even long stretches of road, trying to devise a Cronenberg Routine that will catch FEMA's eye.

People around here don't need to be told twice that opportunities like this come rarely, if ever. A life as the New Cronenberg is considerably more than most, even the affluent, would've allowed themselves to dream for their children.

The school hangs a huge CLOSED sign over its front door, while a series of banners counting down the days appears over Sacrifice Square.

Teenagers work unsupervised in ankle-length JNCO shorts and basketball jerseys, the air around them tangy with sweat and smoke. Lots of small animals suffer—moles, lizards, sparrows—since people have the idea that torturing living but non-human bodies will bring them closer to Cronenberg in FEMA's eyes. They implant these moles, lizards, and sparrows with household chemicals and stray bits of trash, metal, fiberglass . . . anything to compromise their biology, to prejudice it toward the toxic, the bionic, the Cronenbergian.

Other children do it to themselves, some even going so far as to poison or amputate their own limbs, or pieces thereof, punching orifices into parts of their bodies where none had been, and never would have been had nature proceeded undisturbed, which in Cronenberg it never does.

I see several girls with dog and cat penises stapled or sewn into their crotches, and wonder whether FEMA will disqualify some of them for infringing on the ideas of others, and, if so, how it will choose.

●

WHEN THE DAY COMES, we all gather in Sacrifice Square, the air hot from the week's wave of immolation. Above the stage, FEMA has hung a banner that reads, "Pageant of the New Cronenberg," already smudged gray with ash.

The applicants are lined up, checking one another out, avoiding eye contact. One mother arrives with a pile of battered VHS tapes spilling out of her arms. "My son's in here," she says, as she kneels to pick up those that have fallen. "Trust me."

●

A SUCCESSION OF CHILDREN PASSES across the stage, yanked by the strings of their parents' aspirations. Though I root for them all, I can already tell some core factor is missing.

Not one of the twenty-two performances I've seen so far strikes a chord. Pastiche and imitation at best, bad slapstick at worst. None of them comes anywhere close to evoking the Greatness of the Master in his Prime. The fundamentally alien nature of physical embodiment feels as abstract to me now as it would if I'd never seen a Cronenberg film.

As the children deploy the acts they've been working on all week, their parents hovering nervously behind them, it feels like they're tracing the outline of the void at whose center resides the essence that summoned *Scanners*, *The Brood*, *Videodrome*, *The Fly*, *Dead Ringers*, *Naked Lunch*, *Spider*, and *Crash* into being . . . and their failure to fill this void only makes the loss more acute. I hadn't felt like crying before, but now I do.

Through my tears, I buy fried broccoli from a stand and eat it over a trash barrel.

●

BY THE TIME I'm finished, FEMA has called off the Pageant, clearing away all the variously costumed and self-mutilated kids and pulling down the banner.

Dalton clambers onstage to beg for a second chance. His feet are lost among fallen animal teeth and fur, bolts and staples, gall and foam rubber, his beak mask askew. He looks more pathetic than I've ever seen him.

"I'm sincerely sorry that what we had to offer wasn't . . . and I agree that it wasn't . . . um . . . but, what I'm trying to say is . . . give us one last chance. Please. Okay? Let's all take a trip over to The Dodge City Annex and see if anyone there is more to your liking. The citizenry is far more characterful. Another spirit resides there. This much I can promise."

Dalton stutters, but he gets it out. He seems disgusted with himself, like it's an admission he's deeply ashamed of having been forced to make. FEMA seems intrigued. It's clearly not in its interest to leave without a few contenders in tow.

●

So, in another procession with all the defeated Cronenberg-hopefuls taking up the rear, we set off, out of Town along a road no one ever uses because it doesn't lead anywhere except to The Dodge City Annex.

The Dodge City Annex

WE REACH The Dodge City Annex, which turns out to be an adjacent, nearly identical Dodge City, except one in which everyone is deformed in some vividly physical or subtly psychological way. It's from here that Branson is said to draw his wildest extras. Perhaps, I think, remembering all the *Unholy Family* I've been watching, it's also here that the fleshed shadows originate, stealing into the Real Dodge City through the unassuming backgrounds of stock TV footage.

The deep question, as Big Pharmakos puts it to me on the walk over, is whether the Annex predates Blut Branson, or vice versa. "A classic chicken-and-egg conundrum, and one whose implications go all the way to the roots of The Dodge City Foundation Mythos: did the freaks in the Annex exist there all along—perhaps they were even created by a pre-Blut visionary whose name is now lost to history—or, and this is the less heretical view, did Blut create them specifically to serve as extras in his films? Did he conjure them from the same Summoning Pit as all his ideas, the Pit that many claim Dodge City itself arose from, and then leave them there, to wander free and reproduce, until such time as he needed them, or their offspring, again? This is the question, and it's a deeply philosophical one. It goes all the way to the root of our fundamental disagreement as to whether anything at all existed here before Blut Branson."

"It is," Big Pharmakos continues, "fundamentally the question of whether Blut Branson and Paul Broth are one being, or two."

"Who?" I ask, but the commotion is now too intense to hear the answer, if there is one. It seems we've arrived.

●

NOW, in the Annex, Dalton fills in more backstory, for FEMA's sake if not for mine. He starts with an account of the

Annex Civic Fund, set up to provide opportunities for its citizenry using interest from the European Fortune, which reverted to the Town after Patka Esterhazy's descendants failed to reach an equitable decision about who was entitled to what. Over the years, Dalton explains, there've been a variety of projects funded this way, all with the aim of affording the citizens of the Annex a standard of living commensurate with that of Dodge City.

Hanging over Sacrifice Square is a banner that reads: "YOU, TOO, DESERVE A CHANCE TO MAKE *VIDEODROME*." Was it hung just now, to please FEMA, or has it always been here, as definitive a feature of the Annex as any other? All around me, I hear mutually exclusive answers to this question being formed and viciously defended.

In the distance, I see the hulk of the State Prison, which farmed me out to work on the Chain Gang early in my time here, in order to resolve the case of my Dead Hand.

As we make our way along the dusty streets, prone bodies complicate our footwork. From the way they're crawling, it's hard to tell if they're living or dead, or neither. A mass of them crawls toward us from the field in front of the Prison, where they organize into a line.

"Ah," Dalton says, trying to appear confident in front of FEMA. "They're lining up in hopes of being chosen as Official Spokesperson for What's Really Going On Here. Each situation in the Annex gets precisely one Official Spokesperson. That's the Law."

Dalton chooses the first in line, at which point the rest fall upon each other in a free-for-all. As we can tell they'll be destroyed soon, we start ignoring them now. The Chosen One begins, shouting over the bloody demise of his brethren:

"So, we all got this grant money to make our own *Videodrome*, you know, from the Civic Fund, and we knew what an opportunity it was for us to be able to make it, and not just go on with our little tiny lives, but then we get sidetracked. Directing made us power-mad. We started to think that if it was possible to know what it felt like to be Cronenberg, it might not be too much to believe that we could find out what it felt like to be immortal. Very quickly, we grew obsessed. The Cronenberg-state came to seem a very long way beneath us, like a stage of evolution that our ancestors had already outgrown."

FEMA types this into its iPad. I recede into a passive state, as if I were watching this all on the TV in my Room, which, I remind myself, I may well be.

"So," the Spokesperson continues, "we were all sweeping our *Videodrome* storyboards into our compost piles of juvenilia when word came to us, via the Annex Internet, that the State Prison was selling off its lethal injection supplies, having chanced upon a "sixth method" that would no longer involve the torments and humiliations of electrocution, beheading, poisoning, firing squads, or hanging.

"One way or another, as these things go, assuming you believe that ideas have an organic life of their own—which, if you don't: goodbye—all of us would-be *Videodrome* Directors became convinced that these deadly chemicals, if administered properly, would confer in body the immortality that had already taken root in our souls."

"A zombification ritual?" FEMA asks, looking up from its iPad.

The Spokesperson, visibly displeased by the interruption, nods. "Correct. Of course, there'd been plenty of word around the Annex as to the misuse of these chemicals in the Prison System, the botcheries, paralyses, etc., but, in the state we were in at that time, this was music to our ears. It meant only one thing to us: *transformation*. We came to believe, abetted as ever by the Internet, that these chemicals were never intended to cause death but rather to transfigure the body and spirit at their most fundamental level, boiling them down to their simplest components so as to start over, at last getting right what biology had for so many millennia gotten wrong."

Dalton can't hide his dismay at being cut out of the conversation. He looks like he knows he could leave now, and FEMA wouldn't even turn to watch him go. Though his power in Dodge City still greatly outstrips my own, I can't help feeling a little sorry for him.

The Spokesperson, shaking off two mouths nibbling his shins, continues, "Each Death Row inmate had his own special brand of lethal-injection chemical, specifically calibrated both to his body and to the moral fiber behind his crime and subsequent reflection upon it. No two doses alike. So, at this point, we underwent a period of interviews and investigations with the inmates, to see which of us fit most perfectly with which of them. The idea was that we'd buy their doses, and they'd go free, living on as us while we became superhuman by injecting ourselves with the chemicals calibrated for them, if you see what I mean. Good news for all involved.

"Anyway," he adds, "I'll fast-forward since I can see you all more or less get the picture. We bought our doses, exhausting our *Videodrome* budgets, and paraded into this field here"— he points at the field that is now littered with bodies in all states of agony—"to administer our doses, separately in the final moment, each of us turned inward, picturing what we'd come to understand as the *locked box of immortal life* behind our hearts, normally stored for subsequent lives, but now about to come unlocked in the midst of this one."

"Needless to say, you found it harder than you'd imagined to administer properly," FEMA presumes.

"Needless to say, indeed. A total disaster, as you can see. Zombification in the lewdest possible sense."

We all look at the field, which is truly a sorry sight. Some zombies lie on their backs and howl at the sun; others dig uncontrollably at the dirt, opening pits that still others fall into. Some are bleeding from their eyes, others from their ears; others look so pale it's as if their blood has turned to water.

"If you're so fucked up, shouldn't you talk weirder?" Dalton interrupts, if only to reinsert himself into the conversation with uncharacteristic coarseness.

FEMA and the Spokesperson ignore him.

The inmates, spared their executions, stumble through the field. They look like they're trying to balance haste with stealth, afraid of drawing attention to themselves. Or else they've simply lost the knack for crossing open space after so long inside.

●

THERE'D BE NO DRAMATIC EXIT from this scene were it not for the guy with the video camera. He appears only belatedly through the desecration, running behind and between the zombies and inmates with his camera rolling, shouting, "Great!! This kind of thing is just great! Let's get even more of that if we can . . ." as if he believes he's directing the scene, everyone behaving according to a script he's written.

"That guy," the Spokesperson sneers, "opted to just still make *Videodrome*. He said it was enough for him."

FEMA nods, checking its iPad and making a few phone calls.

●

"GREAT," it finally says. "Forgive us if our tastes skew traditional, but we'll take him. In terms of delivering a New Cronenberg to the people, finding one who's actually willing to still make *Videodrome*, in spite of everything, will save us a world of paperwork."

"Very well," the Spokesperson replies, like a slaver at an auction who's just made a sale. "I'll bag him up and bring him over."

B-Movies vs. B-Moves:

A Stranger's Tale

DEJECTED BY **FEMA'S CRASS** and literal-minded decision—who needs another *Videodrome* when the original is streaming in perpetuity?—we march out of the Annex and back to Dodge City. It's still a procession, though hardly a Pageant this time, as all the children mope along in their disheveled costumes, and assorted inmates from the State Prison filter into our midst, their hungry gazes dripping across our exposed skin.

Dissent multiplies as we walk. I hear half the people around me insisting that FEMA created the whole Annex as a ruse, conscripting Dalton as their patsy, to make the voting seem fair when, in reality, all they'd ever intended was to replace the old Cronenberg with an exact replica. "The Illusion of Free Will," I hear a woman to my left mutter. "What else is new?"

●

THE FIRST THING WE SEE upon passing back through the Outskirts is a savage killing on the street outside the Dead Mall, in which a local chapter of the Boys' Boys whips a teenager to death for having had a mother and thus being, as they put it, "born of woman and dead to us."

●

I HURRY BACK to the Hotel just as the *Unholy Family* crew shows up to film the aftermath. Turning on my TV, it appears I've missed the segment about the murder.

The next one focuses on how a new operation has moved into Town: a studio that claims the ability to generate concepts for forty B-Movies a day, dwarfing Blut Branson's Grindhouse Sausage Factory, which has been producing twenty B-Movies a day for, as the newscaster puts it, "longer than you or I can remember."

Blut's grindhouse studio, a subsidiary of his larger enterprise, is responsible for Dodge City classics like *Toe Bath*, in which a pedicure salon that offers clients the opportunity to immerse their feet in tanks where fish nibble dead skin turns bloody when the fish develop a taste for human pus after drinking one client's open sore. Then there's *A/C Man*, in which a poorly installed A/C unit falls from a window onto a man's head, but instead of killing him, it turns him into an A/C-headed monster, breathing Freon and seeking revenge upon the dwellers of the window from which the unit fell, except, being unable to see, he kills everyone in the city before succumbing to global warming in a Texaco restroom. There's also *Wart Benjamin*, which, depending on whom you ask, is either about "a wart that thinks he's a man," or "a wart that splits in two."

The thing is, as the newscaster puts it, "Branson's twenty-B-Movies-a-day studio actually produces all twenty every day, whereas the new forty-B-Movies-a-day studio promises to generate forty concepts a day, but to produce nothing."

This leads to a Schism, which Professor Dalton, who's been lying low since his humiliation at the hands of FEMA—it feels as though a substantial amount of time has already passed since then—is called upon to mediate. Scratching a new beard and yawning like whoever summoned him interrupted a long nap, he wonders aloud, inside the DCTV studio, what the people of Dodge City actually want from their B-Movies at this point in history. "Perhaps," he speculates, "glutting on concepts without the time-sink of watching their consequences will free our brains of the sludge that's been slowing us down. Instead of always feeling like we're behind in our effort to watch twenty B-Movies a day, perhaps now we'll feel like we're way ahead, having scanned forty concepts before breakfast."

To which an off-screen voice retorts, "Yeah, but why even call it a Movie if it isn't one?"

●

IN RESPONSE TO THIS, a stranger comes onscreen and puts forth that what's really important now is not B-Movies at all, but what he calls *B-Moves*, which are instances of B-Movie behavior divorced from the strictures of cinema, brought all the way into real life, "where the rest of us are anyway."

He holds up a laminated sheet showing an introductory set of two hundred B-Moves, which, he promises, "anyone can master with an afternoon of practice."

"Why sit in front of a screen when you could, you know, put your hands right in it?" he wonders rhetorically, and even Dalton has to admit it's a good question.

●

LATER THAT NIGHT, as I'm making a rare jaunt down to the Bar for beer and a soft pretzel, I see the stranger lurking by the rack of tourist brochures. After I strike up a tentative conversation with him, expressing interest in learning a few B-Moves myself, he offers to treat me to dinner. I accept.

"Traveling the country espousing the end of cinema is actually just my day job," he confesses, after our food arrives. "I am, at heart, a Movie freak like all of you. My real passion is the incomparably transgressive Korean cinema of Kim Ki-Duk, whose name I hesitate even to invoke. *The Isle*, *Pieta*, *Mobius* . . . see for yourself. After years of effort, I've transposed myself into his American Avatar. All Asian Directors have American Avatars, just as all Jewish Directors have Gentile Avatars, and vice versa, as you surely know. Each is, to be fair, merely a shadow of the original, but still . . ."

He's beaming, almost crying, as he takes out his phone to show me a rough cut of what he considers his first film as the American Kim Ki-Duk.

I lean in, allowing him to place wireless headphones in my ears while his film plays. It features a male and female lead, both of whom do look like Americanized versions of Korean actors. It's a husband and wife facing hard times, living in a very small apartment, the type that I believe is or was sometimes called a council flat, by those brave souls still residing in the U.K.

The couple's options are severely reduced by poverty, dipping to zero. They maintain their dignity in the face of a corrupt system that manifests little concern for their wellbeing, but it's clear that something's got to give.

With a heavy heart, after having slept on it for a night and taken a long, cold shower in the morning, the wife decides to turn to prostitution. The husband stays in bed until she's left for the day, unable to bear the sight of her in her new professional attire.

The stranger looks up to make sure I'm riveted. I make sure to look like I am.

IN THE NEXT SCENE, the wife returns dejected, beaten down not by the relentlessness of the sex market but by the opposite: no customers all day. Not even any rate inquiries. "I just hung out by myself," she admits. "On the corner outside Denny's."

The husband covers his face at this news, at first relieved and then humiliated in a new way.

THE DAYS GO ON in this pattern. Then, on a tear one night, the husband chances upon a new, even more desperate solution: he'll buy her services himself.

"This is what it's come to," he says sternly, taking out his wallet and asking what she charges.

She tells him, he pays, and they do everything he wants for forty minutes, which involves several trips to the microwave and the letting loose of the contents of a packet labeled Hot Antzz.

That night ends.

●

A WEEK GOES BY like this, the husband buying his wife every night, sometimes twice a night, looking away from the bruises complicating her surface. Then, since this influx of cash is most welcome but not yet sufficient, the wife proposes the inevitable second step: she'll buy her husband, as well. Let him see how it feels.

After some thought, he acquiesces, telling her his rate and beginning to strip. Taking up the broom and metal pan from beside the fireplace, she barks, "Get in there," pointing at the chest where the firewood is kept and scorpions have been known to roost.

After pleading and receiving a severe blow to the ribs, the husband crawls inside, jabbed all the while by his wife, who's paying good money for the privilege. The scorpions seem to multiply through contact with his gonads.

●

BACK AND FORTH and back and forth this goes, the husband buying the wife and the wife buying the husband, until they're both rich, degraded, and terrified of one another. Then the credits roll.

●

"AND SO, the really provocative thing about this film," the stranger begins, removing my earbuds and taking the liberty of discussing his own work as if it were someone else's, "is how the central mystery is never solved: that of where the money comes from. And isn't that just like life? We get by somehow, most of us, but we don't know how. We worry almost to death about not surviving, and yet somehow, semi-magically, we do.

"Now, there are several interpretations that the Director invites us to consider: is there a second couple, identical but for its wealth, inserting itself between the primary couple, and paying for the services rendered? Or are the husband and wife simply able to manifest more money, when thus obliged, than they believed themselves capable of manifesting at the outset? Or, and this is my personal favorite interpretation, is the Director inviting us to consider a more metaphysical possibility, a deeper conflation of the degrading effects of prostitution and economic striving, such that by simple virtue of crossing this line with each other, sacrificing the very last shreds of their dignity, the husband and wife conjure money out of the ether, calling it forth from the very shame they've descended into, as if the core sexuality of prostitutes naturally yielded cash rather than children?"

He goes on in this vein as I creep toward the edge of the booth, trying to time my exit for the moment just before he cues up the next film on his phone, which I can tell is about to happen.

"Prison Pics":

Unholy Family Season Finale

DRUNK AFTER MY VIEWING SESSION in the Bar, in which I drained several beers but failed to touch my food, I return to my Room and turn on the TV just in time to catch the *Unholy Family Season Finale*. What with the Cronenberg emergency and the sudden intrusion of the American Kim Ki-Duk—or perhaps simply because time accelerates as one gets older—the season has flown by. I promised myself I'd revisit the question of what to do with my life as soon as the season was over, so, though I wish it wasn't, it seems like the time's almost here.

The *Finale* is billed as an "exposé of Dodge City's little known, viciously cutthroat Art World, an even higher-stakes version of its notoriously cutthroat Film Industry."

"In the course of my wanderyears following the dissolution of an unsuccessful anal marriage to a nun and the crossing of God's DNA with mine—she was, you see, vaginally married to the Lord at the same time," the episode's narrator begins, his voice strikingly similar to that of the stranger who just took me to dinner, "I was imprisoned in one of the Towns I passed through. Hard to say which one. When you live a life like mine, they all start to look the same."

I open a minibar mezcal and resign myself to whatever story he's about to tell.

"Anyway, it was one of those situations," he continues, "where I hadn't actually committed the crime they booked me for, but since there were so many crimes from previous Towns that I had—and had gotten away with—it seemed fair to do some time here. Kind of make up for them all in one fell swoop, you know?"

I nod.

"So, they locked me away in the State Prison, on the far side of The Dodge City Annex, and I thought that was it, like a life sentence. They wanted to watch me rot, more for who I was than for what I'd done."

He pauses here long enough that I feel compelled to nod again.

"I started doing my time, untroubled until photos of me in there, deep in my cell, surfaced on the Internet. A woman from the apartment tower next door had been photographing me, shooting straight into the Prison from her balcony."

●

AS THE NARRATOR DRAGS his story out, I sink into The Dodge City Private Internet, picking the story up there, looking at the Prison pics on my laptop while listening to him describe them.

In the pics, he looks much younger but not much healthier than he does on TV. I keep scrolling through them and reading digests of what happened:

Petra Mance, who lived in the apartment tower next to the Prison, started out taking pictures of all the prisoners, in the most predictably compromising positions—shower stuff, beat-off stuff, submission and punishment stuff, whatever she could manage through the windows. Her aim in those days was low.

"But something more profound manifested in the shots of this prisoner: total resignation covered his face like an acne out-break, an apartness from the usual grim flux of prison life, too sad and peaceful to be called despair, though it certainly wasn't enlightenment. More like the profound knowledge that he was right where he deserved to be, in a cell the size of all the space he deserved on this planet after all the waste he'd laid to the spaces he'd passed through on his way there . . . and a humble, almost reverential acceptance of this knowledge," as Mance put it in her artist's statement, once the Art World got involved. "A sort of beatification through confinement, the limits of his soul expressed in terms of the limits of his cell. A man who knew he had God in him and yet had used that God for nothing but the most predictable sort of debasement. And so now, behind bars, he was sweating that God to the surface. Letting it out any way he could, before it turned to cancer in his bowels."

●

SOON, collectors were pouring into Dodge City, eager to get close to the source, in on the ground floor.

When the demand to possess this prisoner in the flesh reached a tipping point, the Art World submitted a petition for his release to the judge who'd put him away. I'm now getting all this from the Internet—the TV is nothing but a soundtrack to my surfing.

The judge, aware that he was being offered a rare chance to dip his toe in Art-World greatness, released the prisoner after taking the minimum requisite time to appear as though he were weighing a grave decision.

When the prisoner got out, the Art World hosted a Release Day Parade in the Annex to welcome its newest celebrity onto the Open Market. The expectation was that he'd take his saintly face on an international tour, posing as a modern-day Augustine, bloated and beatific with a Dead God decaying in his soft tissue.

●

BUT, as soon as he was prepped for his first junket in Paris, he reverted. He simply went back to how he'd been before his arrest, like he'd been on pause the whole time. "A textbook recidivist," as one article puts it. "Same as all the others."

The beatitude that had crowded his face when he was alone in his cell facing a lifetime of menacing solitude cleared up overnight, and the full skeeze of his previous self seeped back in.

As the Art World had no use for a man like this, he was put back in jail, this time in a deeper, darker cell with no photographic access from the outside.

Petra Mance was likewise let go. She pulled a Jerzy Kosinski soon thereafter, suffocating herself with a plastic bag. Her Suicide note read, simply, "Whoever finds my body—take some pics and see if they're worth anything?"

This, a number of articles agree, epitomized the rise and fall of The Dodge City Art World. "We are, simply put, a Movie Town, not an art one. We're no Marfa," says Dalton, when I look back at the TV. "We worship Blut Branson for a reason. The repeatability of cinema, the way in which thousands of people can witness the same spectacle for $10 a ticket, rather than a single collector owning the entire thing for $10 million: this is where our center of gravity lies, and always will."

●

THE QUESTION OF HOW the prisoner, supposedly still locked in the depths of the State Prison, managed to tell his story to the *Unholy Family* crew is also, I think, answerable only in cinematic terms. No shortage of Impersonators around here; no end of reenactment. I resume my web search, unearthing a cache of photos of photorealistic paintings, rich and unstinting as the best of Gerhard Richter, of this prisoner locked in yet-deeper solitude, so deep inside that no light can penetrate, as if his cell and his body have merged completely, and I skim articles claiming that these paintings are the true prize of the Art World, the entire story of the earlier photographs and of Petra Mance's ostensible Suicide told only, and apocryphally, to inflate the value of her paintings, the best ever produced in Dodge City, but I drift to sleep before I can get anywhere near the bottom of it.

PHASE II:

Inklings

Pilot Season

A LOW PERIOD FOLLOWS, one of senseless ambient clicking now that *Unholy Family*'s over for the season. The thought of there being nothing more to watch is discomfiting. Though I know I promised myself I would revisit the hard questions as soon as the season ended, I find I'm too scattered to make any headway just yet.

Instead, I drift deeper into the mysteries of the online Art World, putting myself in the position of that prisoner in his unlit solitude, identifying with his condition in the paintings that may or may not exist to a degree that I wish I could downplay, if only to myself. "Nothing to see here, folks," I whisper, in bed.

●

A SCREAMING THROUGH MY WINDOW pulls me out of the click trance. I peer out to see Professor Dalton shouting from a dais in Sacrifice Square, set up in the foundation of the toppled Cronenberg effigy.

Adorned in his beak mask, he shouts, "On this day of all days, *Unholy Family* is hosting a one-time-only shot at creating a brand-new series in lieu of their regular programming for next year. In other words, Pilot Season is open!"

I find myself wondering if the show's foray into reality TV sputtered out sooner than anticipated, or if this is merely its next phase.

"One week from today," Dalton continues, "all of you are to submit your concepts to me, and the best will be vetted by *Unholy Family* itself, and aired next season. All of Dodge City will know your name. You will, at long last, be famous!"

●

SO, it's finally time to write something. At this point, I tell myself, it would be indefensible not to. I open my laptop and type the words, "Get to work."

●

AND I DO. I emerge in the Square a week later with two ideas jotted on notecards, one series per pocket. Both are vetoed. By evening, they've narrowed it down to:

All High-School Bands Get Huge (Big Pharmakos): A version of Dodge City in which any group of teenagers even remotely resembling a band is immediately launched into Springsteen-levels of fame, even before playing a single show or recording a single track. One practice, or even the rumor of a practice, is enough to make them their generation's Ramones. Take any two kids whose parents got them electric guitars for their sixteenth birthdays and put them in a room together . . . and the Greil Marcus book writes itself. The reoccurring conflict of the series is the impossibility of making this happen. No one is willing or able to form a high-school band, even considering the obscene profit margin and the ironclad assurance of a lifetime of adulation. The series follows numerous botched attempts to get two or more high schoolers together for a single jam session in someone's basement one weekend night when there's nothing else to do.

All Body Moistures Run Dry (Gottfried Benn): A version of Dodge City in which all our bodies have gone dry, because, as the German poet's tagline reads, "we over-basted ourselves in our own juices when we were young." No one is able to have pleasurable sex anymore—only procreative, with awful friction—and no one is able to speak except in a lizardy rasp. Unable to sweat, we faint at least once a day. Some clerics claim we are still wet on the inside, deeper in than any mortal implement can reach, but, nevertheless, we suffer from the "bloat of unreleased energies," our skin always about to burst, like turkeys crackling in the oven . . . until one member of the community discovers a well in a disused utility shed that contains precisely one drop of moisture for each citizen. In a democratic society, each citizen would choose when and how to use this drop, but in the Dodge City of Benn's proposed series, a small consortium of developers takes it all, ritually fucking and spitting on one another thousands of times, while everyone else further mummifies, in a "reimagining of *Chinatown* that is barely a reimagining at all."

And *Taking the Rap* (The Artist Formerly Known as The Night Crusher): A version of Dodge City in which one guy kills another for no reason. This guy, after sleeping on it, decides he isn't ready for Death Row. So, he calls his friend and asks if he'll take the rap for him. The friend says okay. In order to make the transference of guilt realistic, they dig up the body and resurrect it. Then, the original murderer turns his back while his friend kills the resurrected victim, making him the genuine murderer. In the next episode, the same thing happens: the now-guilty friend phones another friend, and they resurrect the body again so that the other friend can kill it and become the guilty one. On and on, each episode featuring one such shunting, until everyone in Town has had a chance to kill the original victim and face Death Row before calling a friend to get out of it. The theory is that the victim can only be resurrected if he's going to be immediately killed again, so there's no net loss from the World of the Dead. But the show takes a turn in Episode 11, when it comes to light that the victim has changed over the course of this round robin—from murder to murder, it hasn't been the same person at all. Perhaps there has never been any resurrection. Perhaps, as Episode 12 speculates, half of Dodge City has simply killed the other half. Certain humanists despair; certain environmentalists rejoice.

The team behind *Unholy Family,* meanwhile, as if to ward off usurpation, pitches its own spinoff series called *Unholy Family: Intermediate Generations*, in which "half-relatives" are inserted between all members of every family: between siblings, between parents and children, between spouses . . . making it such that no lines of heredity are direct. Now, all lines are mediated through strangers, to be played by extras from the Annex, attenuating the lines of familial connection by their inexplicable presence and refusal to leave, lingering interminably "between every man, woman, and child and their Maker."

●

THIS IDEA DRUMS UP some interest, but the overall sentiment is that *Unholy Family* itself, still running after longer than most of our lifetimes, scratches enough of its own itches as is. Thus —and here again I find it hard to believe in the uniqueness of this outcome—*Unholy Family* is renewed for another season, and no new show is allowed on the air.

"Perhaps," I tell Big Pharmakos at the Bar after voting has wound down, "they simply do it to shore up power. You know? To remind us that we don't want real change. Don't you think?"

"Think what?" he asks, fixated on the Bar's TV as *Unholy Family* broadcasts the scene we've just witnessed as a bonus episode to tide us over until the new season begins.

Finger Torture:
A Prophetic Dream

I T'S BEEN A LONG DRY SPELL in which *Unholy Family* has continually aired reruns while working on its new season. These reruns, delving as they do into the evergreen question of where people come from, stir the cauldron of Dodge City's innumerable and mutually inconsistent Origin Stories, keeping us all piqued with the promise of a unifying explanation.

Deep in this period, I dream I'm watching an episode called "Finger Torture," about a guy who, believing that his dreams have prepared him for torture, signs up to be a Scarecrow, which is someone who is hired to be tortured in place of someone who can't take it. The idea is that the Scarecrow will either withstand the torture with a modicum of dignity intact, or else determine that it's excessive and lucidly deliver the information the torturer is after, rather than regressing into the histrionics of a Scared Crow, as those who melt under the torture for which they have been singled out are called, according to the episode's prologue.

"In those days of sudden, random torture in Dodge City," concludes the narrator, "the Scarecrow business was unsurprisingly booming."

The guy who volunteers to be a Scarecrow claims he's had a series of dreams in which a duo breaks into his room and removes his fingers joint by joint, night after night, each time more painful than the last, because his fingers have regrown imperfectly in the interim, but also each time less traumatic, because he's been conditioned to expect it. This, I believe, is the distinction that anesthesiologists draw between 'pain' and 'hurt.' Though I can't remember which is which, one refers to an unpleasant physical sensation, the other to the resulting awareness that something bad is occurring to the body.

"Indeed, finger torture was the only thing my dreams had made me ready for," this character tells the camera from behind a veil, his voice distorted to protect his identity.

●

AT THIS POINT, I slip away from dreaming that I'm watching *Unholy Family* and into dreaming that the events are happening to me, and not for the first time. Now, a guy and a girl in matching blue T-shirts and khaki work pants turn on the lights in my Room and pull me up in bed, stuffing my reading pillow under my back, so I don't slump over when they let go.

Then they begin cutting my fingers joint by joint, starting with the thumb of my left hand and working toward the pinky of my right. First the guy slices the pads of the fingertips with a serrated bread knife, then the girl cuts off the joints with a pair of garden shears.

"Is the code a woman's name? Is it Heather? Is the dial really a switch?" Every night, they ask these same three questions.

Without giving me a chance to respond, the guy slices the skin on all my second joints, and the girl comes through with the shears. Then it's on to my third joints, until all thirty are in a pile in my lap. They spritz the pile with a water bottle like it's seeds they expect to grow.

Before the shock hits me, I tunnel into my head, into a dream within the dream, which I perceive as a daydream since in the dream I don't know I'm dreaming. The place I'm trying to reach is the parking lot behind the Hotel. In the daydream, I elbow the Hotel's back door open with minimal effort, my fingers provisionally reattached, and step out into the lot, where two maids are smoking, oblivious to the gasps still coming from my Room.

I feel like one member of a duo who's left his partner behind— I know that someone is being tortured in my bed, but I no longer feel like it's me.

I hurry across the parking lot, past the outdoor laundry station

and the shattered vending machine and the pool with its de-
flated raft, and dive into a waiting limo. As I buckle my seat-
belt, a hooded boss beside me asks, "Do you have it?"

I say "Yes," and hold out my hands. The fingers fall into his
leather kit bag. Once he's zipped them up, we cruise along
Sunset Boulevard to a bank deposit box, where I get out and
dump the bag in.

"The balance is in your account," whispers the boss through
the tinted window, not letting me back in. "Now, you're ready
for L.A."

Return to Branson Mansion

NOW THAT I'M READY for L.A., I climb into the Hollywood Hills. Soon, I'm near the top, looking down over the lighted bowl of the city, before I remember that I've been here before, back when that black limo drove me to dinner at what I'd been told was Branson Mansion.

No sooner does that phrase enter my consciousness than I'm again walking up the torchlit drive, past the hedges and the carriage house and the fountain out front—was there a fountain last time?—and knocking on the front door, though I don't have an invite this time.

The door creaks open, and I tiptoe in, removing my shoes and continuing barefoot across the cold tile and hardwood floors. I consider whispering, "Hello," but think better of it, deciding simply to look around instead, taking my chances in these rooms that may or may not be empty, and, if they're not empty, may or may not be inhabited by another version of myself. I feel emboldened by the finger torture, at last prepared to face whoever's lurking here.

I wander the echoing hallways, past bookshelves lined with Hungarian, Turkish, Maltese, and Swiss editions of *Branson on Branson: The Master Speaks*, and into the kitchen, where the outlines of Blut and his wife or mistress sit in chairs, hovering in the half-light, like they're being projected from an unseen source in the walls.

I know better than to approach them. Instead, I take a bottle of Cava from the fridge—my fingers have regrown once again —and begin to explore the back rooms, those I didn't see last time, swigging as I go.

●

MEMORIES STIR, faint inklings of my childhood spent in thrall to Movies, watching four or five a day, then bundling them up and bringing them back to the Movie Store and exchanging them for four or five more, in lieu of any schooling. In lieu even, it seems, of any parenting or formative friendships.

And then, seamlessly, I began to direct: Movies started seeping out of me, without any concerted effort, without any real planning, just an ironclad symbiosis between my imagination and the materials of the outside world. I etched my vision onto celluloid with all the power of a natural disaster, inherent and unstoppable, until I grew powerful enough to build this Mansion and fill it with my presence.

I'm sweating now, upstairs in the Master Bathroom, running a bath in the gigantic jet-equipped tub. I strip naked, feeling my chest and stomach as if they were Branson's, and sink into the water up to my neck, eyes closed, so deep in the fantasy of being Blut Branson, having long ago become Dodge City's Undisputed Cinematic Overlord, that I don't notice myself passing out in the heat.

Regression Pills:
A Dream of My First Movie

I COME-TO, spluttering in the bathwater. I want to stay in, but feel so dizzy I can tell it's not a good idea. So, I towel off, put on a B.B.-embossed robe I find hanging behind the door, and shuffle down the hall to the Master Bedroom, where I pull the robe off and flop naked and still damp onto Branson's memory-foam mattress. It caves in to accept me, pulling me deep into a dream it must've been waiting to share.

●

IN THE DREAM, I have just finished directing my first Movie. It stars a pedophile on a regimen of highly specialized psychotropic drugs. The moral premise is that pedophiles and child molesters are radically different beasts: both have the same innate, societally abhorrent urge, but one resists it with all its might, while the other gives in, either gladly or under internal duress. The first category, according to the film's drowsy narrator, "is to be commended for its efforts to deny its basic wiring, while the second is to be punished to the full extent of the Law."

The name of the male lead is George; the female lead is Chloë. George, a pedophile of the type that's determined to deny its wiring, has been prescribed a trial dose of a psychotropic drug designed to induce temporary hallucinations in which adults appear to him as children, so that he might perform the typical sex act with a consenting adult while at the same time accessing the sense of peace and inner wholeness that only sex with a child can offer him.

The plot twist comes early: Chloë—who, until now, has been unaware of her boyfriend's practice of selectively transforming her into a little girl—accidentally ingests one of his pills, left out on the bathroom sink, believing it to be one of the anti-depressants that she has long insisted she doesn't take, but in fact always leaves out on the bathroom sink in order to take just before sex, when she needs them most.

When she returns to the bedroom and witnesses George trans-forming into a little boy, she is, not being a pedophile herself, shaken up. She pulls away, desperate to find her bearings in a room that's closing in on her, fast ceasing to feel like home.

She crawls backward, as George—fully-aroused at the sight of her as a child, still under the impression that all is proceeding as usual—pursues, knocking her into a bookcase that falls on them both, rendering them unconscious for a five-minute per-iod of dead-silent screen time.

●

WHEN THEIR CONSCIOUSNESSES RESUME, the two have en-tered an almost-sweet regression to early childhood infatua-tion, though fraught in this case with the memory of inter-course rather than of a faint, unvoiced premonition thereof.

Not only do they look like children to each other, but, thanks to their shared perspective on the other's regression, they now feel like children, as well. Like a coed sleepover slipping off the rails, I think, as if explaining my film to that stranger I met in the Hotel Bar, after he's watched it on my phone.

●

THE MIDDLE ACT FINDS THEM in a state close to bliss, living in their apartment as if it belonged to a much-older cousin, someone cool and grown-up and out of town, who would be glad to guide them through the mysteries they're just starting to long to explore, if only he or she were present.

They raid the pantry for Frosted Flakes and Swiss Miss, acting like they're on the world's longest snow day and nothing's impossible.

My dreaming attention phases in and out during this section, as I'm both watching and directing the film at the same time.

Part of me is waiting for the other shoe to drop, while part of me fears it never will or that it already has. I'm wondering if the pill she took will eventually wear off, and she'll be forced to watch George revert to being a man, like some terrible switch-out has occurred and she's now in a situation she very much shouldn't be in, while he goes on taking the pills so that she remains child-sized in his eyes, or if they'll both grow addicted, endlessly re-upping their newfound perspective on each other, until one or both overdoses, if that's possible in this case, or until their supply runs out, which surely one day it must.

Perhaps an excess of these pills will culminate only in a mutual regression to apparent infancy, each squinting in the dark to make the other out, like those fetuses in the brine tank from the *Unholy Family Season Premiere.*

●

WHAT ACTUALLY HAPPENS comes from further afield, drawing me back out of myself for the third act. Chloë grows so overcome with terror at the conflicted nature of her relationship with this man she sees as a boy that she becomes convinced he has killed her father:

THE ONLY REASONABLE CONCLUSION SHE COULD'VE COME TO!!

reads an unexpected title card in the center of the screen.

This Dead Father, the narrator informs us, is none other than George, the man she used to live with and now cannot find.

Falling into her psychic disturbance, the boy-George mimics her fear, behaving as though his mother, Chloë, is also gone, replaced by this girl-child he can't help but lust after, despite the competing depth of his desire to wail in her arms.

The memory of their parents lingers in the apartment, growing so oppressive it forces them out into the hallway.

●

NOW, the climactic journey begins. They fall to roaming the massive apartment complex, charging from room to room, knocking on doors, squeaking in baby voices at the neighbors, begging to be taken in or given a clue as to the nature of their orphanhood:

ALONE AND UNLOVED!!

reads another title card. By this point, they've taken on the roles of brother and sister, a gumshoe duo keen to solve the mystery of their parents' disappearance.

It's a tribute to my generosity of spirit, as a Director, that I never have them turn hostile and assign blame to each other. They remain united in their search, convinced that a tragedy has befallen them both in equal measure, scouring the building from top to bottom, then spilling out into Dodge City, off the screen, which remains blank, since the dream has ended.

●

AS I SLEEP, I hear them knock on my door, as I knew eventually I would. It's either them, I think, or it's Blut and his wife or mistress coming to bed after a long night out. Either way, I resign myself to my fate and ask them to come in.

They do, looking exhausted and shaken up. I put the kettle on to boil, though I have no teabags or instant coffee to offer, and wait for the boiler to click before asking the question that's been on the tip of my tongue since they arrived, which is, "Got any more of those pills?"

I'm afraid they're about to say, "What pills?" but instead they nod, and each hands me one, from separate vials, like they'd each had their own prescription all along.

"Are you our father?" they ask, and I realize, with the pills on my tongue, that their doses are wearing off. Soon, I'll see them as children, but they'll see me and each other as the adults that none of us wants to be.

"Not for long," I answer, getting up, taking a new pill from each of their vials, and placing them on their tongues like communion wafers. Then I take the kettle off the boiler and pour three mugs of hot water for us to wash the pills down with.

A Hurried Return to Dodge City

I WAKE in the blazing sun in Branson Mansion, queasy as I remember the Movie I dreamed up last night, though also excited about what it portends. It's derivative of *Unholy Family*, I think, but there's something original there, too. Some small spark of selfhood that mustn't be extinguished.

Afraid of falling into a yet-stranger dream, I hurry downstairs, still naked, and out the door, planning to hustle all the way down into L.A. to begin my Life in Movies, as so many have done before me, when the black limo pulls up and opens its back door, and I have no choice but to get in.

"You're late," the driver says, rolling down the partition. "Put these on." He tosses a bundle through. Then he rolls the partition back up.

Unwrapping the bundle, I see a pair of starched blue pants, white boxer-briefs, a white T-shirt, a blue dress shirt, and a black blazer. Awkward as the maneuver is, especially since we're now winding down Mulholland Drive and back to Dodge City, I manage to put on the outfit, surprised at how well it fits, despite the fact that my body still looks child-sized to me.

Just as I finish pulling the blazer over my shoulders and adjusting the sleeves of the dress shirt underneath, the driver rolls the partition back down and says, "Okay, sir, we're here."

Letting myself slip into a fantasy where it's now the opening night of *Regression Pills*, I exit the limo in the heart of Sacrifice Square, onto a rope-lined red carpet mobbed with paparazzi.

PHASE III:

The Blut Branson

Retrospective

(Watching Movies)

The Retrospective Begins

I PUSH MY WAY UP the red carpet, through the paparazzi glare, still imagining I'm the Guest of Honor, about to make my world-historical début.

I'm climbing the front steps of the Temple when I spot Big Pharmakos in the crowd. He nods when he sees me, expressing approval though not surprise at my luxe outfit. He is likewise dressed in slacks and a blazer, tight over his gargantuan frame, and he's back in his lizard-skin cowboy boots, which I haven't seen him wear since his comedy career hit a wall and he turned Right.

"Once per year," Big Pharmakos whispers as we take our seats, and I know he's about to kill my fantasy and put me back in my place, "the Temple shows all of Branson's 'secular films,' meaning those not deemed too holy for public consumption. Given that all, even these secular titles, are too holy to be issued on video and certainly too holy for streaming, this Retrospective is the only way to see them. It's a sister-Ritual to the Purge of the Impersonators, a Part II to that Ritual's Part I."

Dalton stands at the front of the auditorium, under the unlit screen, like a cantor about to remove a Holy Scroll from its protective Ark. He clears his throat as the sold-out audience finds its seats.

When the last stragglers are seated, he begins, "Welcome, People of Dodge City. I would say it's great to see so many of you here, but of course where else would you be?"

Muted laughter in the auditorium.

"I'll tell you where: nowhere at all. The notion of skipping the Blut Branson Retrospective, of simply *opting out*, is comprehensible solely on the level of a thought experiment. It makes no more sense than this age-old question: 'if God can do anything, can He build a rock too heavy for Him to lift?' The answer, in that case, is obviously both yes and no. In this case, as you are all well aware, the answer is even simpler. It is, quite simply indeed, yes and yes. Yes, I will attend. Yes, here you all are. Needless to say, there will be no intermission. Think of Wagner at Bayreuth. Think of that, then multiply it by a thousand, then think of God, and then . . . well, anyway, there will be no intermission. Enjoy." Dalton bows as the screen behind him flickers to life.

●

I'D FOUND a pen and notepad in the inside pocket of my blazer, but both were confiscated at the door. "No Graven Images allowed," I was told, so what follows are my recollections of what I saw, written in my Room later in the night—or after several nights, depending on how much external time passed during the Retrospective—though whether I adequately saw these titles, or rather fell into a trance as soon as the lights went down and dreamed up Movies of my own, is more than a Drifter like me can say.

The Murder of Nicola Teensmah

*T*HE MURDER OF NICOLA TEENSMAH, Branson's first known film, tells the devastatingly simple story of a man whose only calling is to kill a child.

This is all that Branson allows us to know about his central figure, whom he calls 'Dan,' a name we only learn from Dan's arrest log after more than thirty minutes of screen time have elapsed. So, this central figure begins life as an unnamed everyman and only upon incarceration does he receive the nearly meaningless moniker he'll casually bear for the rest of our time with him.

In the film's opening scenes, we see the-man-not-yet-named-Dan going quietly insane in an unremarkable Southern California apartment—shot presumably in the Desert outside Dodge City—picking things up and putting them down, staring at the clock, grazing from the refrigerator, all while drawing picture after picture with the caption *The Murder of Nicola Teensmah*. These pictures are powerful, but more disturbed than disturbing, a mess of mutilated child bodies that never achieves the frigid aesthetic cohesion of dedicated psychopathy.

These early scenes present an absolutely convincing portrait of fantasy wearing itself down, as our man approaches the point at which he will be compelled to do the thing he has for so long nursed in ideation, laboriously shunting his compulsion into the symbolic.

"No!" the thing inside him finally shouts. "No more postponement. No more representation. The time has come for you to make me real."

●

THE DECISIVE MOMENT ARRIVES when his neighbor, with whom we've seen him interact once before, dies and leaves him her modest fortune, which he uses to quit the office job where we've seen him sitting at his desk, slowly cutting the flesh behind his knee with an index card. Untethered from any normalizing routine, he enters an excruciating funk in his apartment, deep in the darkness of the one room that is not his bedroom.

In a shot that strikes me as quintessential Branson, a ray of light glints off the man-soon-to-be-named-Dan's left eye in such a way that it remains unclear whether he has generated this light or is reflecting it from some trans-dimensional source. To anyone who's seen a Branson film before, there can be no question that a grave decision is in the process of being made. When the light stops glinting, he stands up and walks to the courthouse.

In the next shot, he is sitting with the county judge, explaining his proposition. "I am willing to spend the majority of my re-maining life in the State Prison for the privilege of murdering a child with impunity upon my release."

"So," the judge replies, while chewing a cigar, "you are, in a sense, conflating the child's death with your own, insofar as you are sacrificing your own life at this relatively early stage in order to efficaciously sacrifice another life when yours has already been squandered, thereby renewing yourself through the child, hoping to be reborn as him in the moment of kill-ing."

"Yes," says our man, cinching the deal.

●

THE SECOND ACT OPENS on Dan in the State Prison, after his name has been revealed on the arrest log, which also reveals that he has been sentenced to forty-seven years.

Dan spends these forty-seven years aging before our eyes, praying to a hand-carved soap statue of the child he will kill upon his release. Forty years into his sentence, with seven to go, he celebrates a quiet birthday alone in his cell, dancing in a circle with the statue in his arms, whispering, "Today you,

Nicola Teensmah, are born. When I am released, you will be seven. Today my life begins in earnest, as well."

As I watch, I imagine Branson alone in his mansion, writing these lines, and I can't help but place myself inside his body, creating a masterpiece that I will affix my name to instead of his. I'm aware that this kind of thinking is only a means of delaying the grim duty of finding my own cinematic language in my own Room upon awakening from this toxic stupor of idol-envy, but it feels too good to stop just yet.

●

WHEN THE DAY OF DAN'S RELEASE ARRIVES, he walks into the blazing sun as a man of seventy-five, played by an actor who appears to be the father of the one who played him before, unless, of course, the film was shot in real time, with a single aging star.

The look on his face conveys relief to be freed undergirded with terror at the fate his younger self has damned him to. In the film's only instance of voiceover, we hear Dan think, "Well, I figured, since I'd invested my life in it, I'd better follow through, though I sure wished I could've taken a pass."

Over the next ten minutes, we watch Dan wander from one drab location to another—a tire shop, a fast-food window, a secondhand clothing market, the gas station where Drifter Jim works—looking people over, holding their gazes too long, daring them to reciprocate. I get the sense that Dan's warning the people of Greater Los Angeles, through a sort of low-grade telepathy, to keep their seven-year-olds away, in what amounts to his first and final attempt at Grace.

And it is as if these people have received the message: no children are seen in this sequence, not even in the background, where they have always been before, seemingly oblivious to the camera, or acting out micro-films of their own, harboring thoughts that the viewer will never be privy to.

●

ONCE DAN'S WANDERINGS HAVE TAKEN HIM as far into the San Fernando Valley as he (and we) can bear to go, he discovers a seven-year-old on the bench of what appears to be a bus stop, though no road passes in front of it.

As a viewer of a film, especially a Branson film, I'm aware that the boy has been posed like this, but, immersed as I am in Dan's perspective at this point, stumbling across the boy feels significantly upsetting, as if he, and he alone, failed to heed the warning.

Next, the boy slides off the bench and follows Dan into the dusty afternoon, deepening toward the west. The screen freezes after they've disappeared around a bend, then cuts to them in a motel room so sparse it barely reads as a motel room at all: there's a mattress with no bedding, a linoleum floor with no carpet, a wall with a single window, and a curtain blocking out the twilight.

As Dan and the boy sit on the mattress, images of a grocery store filter in, like the two of them are processing their memories of shopping in lieu of facing the future. We see Dan picking up packaged cakes and holding them out to the boy, enticingly, almost begging him to accept these treats in a reversal of the typical interaction wherein the son demands what the father insists he cannot have.

The boy simply nods, holding the cakes like the inanimate objects they are. At the checkout counter, the teenager ringing them up smiles and says, "Your grandfather must really love you."

Without making eye contact, the boy mumbles, "He's my father."

●

WHEN BRANSON CUTS BACK to the motel room, Dan is crying. He looks at the boy, turning his back on the camera, demanding privacy.

Then he reaches under the mattress and pulls out a long,

curved boning knife. Branson offers no explanation of how it came to be here; he knows that by now his audience is past the point of expecting realism to spare us what's coming. Dan waves it through the air, trying to get the boy's attention. The boy stares downward, seeing the knife when it passes through his line of sight but making no effort to follow it.

Dan grows increasingly livid. "Look at me!" he finally shouts, revealing how very long it's been since he has spoken. "You are Nicola Teensmah. I'm sorry, but you are. My first, and last, best friend. And for that you must suffer. If I did not do what I'm about to do, what happened when we were kids would keep happening, on and on through the ages, to both of us in every form we ever took."

His voice falls to a whisper, as if he's trying not to hear himself. The knife, stretched like a placenta between their bellies, shimmers.

A howling creeps under the frozen image before Branson cuts to paramedics kicking down the door. Inside, the devastation is so complete it remains indescribable for several seconds.

When I'm finally able to make sense of the room's interior, all I see is the boy drenched in blood, leaning on the long knife like a cane. There's something old about him, but I can't identify what it is. It's as if Branson has filmed the boy's essence, capturing the wizened ghost inside.

The paramedics approach warily at first, but Nicola Teensmah is beyond violence. There's no sign of a second body, and there's no sound until the boy says, his voice clear and even, "My name is Nicola Teensmah, and I'm ready to spend my life in jail."

●

HERE THE SCREEN FREEZES again, the boy's face slowly turning into that of the young Dan, from the film's opening, indicating the completion of some awful cycle whose nature the audience can never hope to comprehend.

And then, as I will come to expect from the films that follow, Dan's face morphs into Branson's, and he says, licking a drop of blood from his lower lip, "At that point, all those years ago, what I suspected but didn't yet know for sure was that I was just getting started. I had an inkling but no hard proof about how much was still to come. Needless to say, the hard proof follows. Enjoy."

Whether this message is part of the original film or an interstitial moment spliced in for the sake of the Retrospective is more than I can say. I can't help but see the film as a metaphor for the admittedly one-sided relationship between Blut and myself, though which of us maps onto Dan and which onto Nicola is more than I feel ready to decide just yet.

The Harmless Slaughterer

B Y THIS POINT in the Retrospective, which has a strict no-reentry policy, meaning that all films must be watched in the gathering haze of those shown before, I'm losing track of the beginnings and endings, and my critical faculties are fading. It's starting to feel like one ultra-long film, which I suspect is Dalton's intention, assuming he's the one who programmed it.

Now I'm watching a pastoral, old-timey version of Dodge City, a little Shtetl-like, as Dodge City's past can sometimes seem—as if the Old Country were located not overseas but deep in the Heart of America—when a Wanderer appears in Town, stealing in under milky cloud cover just before dawn, skulking among the pastures like a warlock in a Hungarian folktale, gaunt and black-cloaked, face obscured under a wide-brimmed felt hat. The camera hangs back as he takes a few preliminary turns around the pens that hold The Dodge City Farm Animals—pigs, sheep, cows, and goats by the looks of it, though I have the impression that some animals are playing others, as is often the case in Branson films, since "casting is ninety-nine percent of directing" is one of his favorite phrases, if *Branson on Branson* is to be believed.

After pausing in what looks like contemplation for a moment, the Wanderer leans down to whisper in one of the animals' ears. As soon as he's finished, the animal—a goat, by the looks of it—yawns exaggeratedly and falls over. At this point, I can't tell if it's supposed to be dead or sleeping.

●

DEAD, as it turns out. Over the next few days, the film reveals the method that the Slaughterer—now that we know what the Wanderer is—uses: he simply strides up to one of the farm animals on his long legs, whispers in its ear, and stands back to watch it gently, even peacefully, keel over.

"What's he whispering?" is, of course, the none-too-subtle subtext of the film at this point. This phrase itself is whispered among the Townspeople, who always populate the backgrounds of Branson's films, played, as ever, by actual Annex citizens.

"What's he whispering?" Indeed. I whisper the phrase in my seat during a montage in which ten or twelve animals are killed in quick succession.

As this montage continues, the Slaughterer—now known as "the Harmless Slaughterer," a phrase whose ambiguity doesn't dawn on me until I reflect on it later, once the fever of the Retrospective has broken—whispers in the ears of all the farm animals of Dodge City, causing them to keel over one by one, until the entire stock of the Town has been reduced to meat, which, according to five or six interview testimonials included in this section of the film, is the sweetest, butteriest, and most delicious they've ever tasted.

"Like goat-lobster," says an old man in overalls with an eyepatch.

●

THE ONLY PROBLEM, of course, is that once all the animals are dead, none are left to kill. At this point, to no one's surprise but to everyone's dismay, the Harmless Slaughterer departs, into the same gray clouds from which he emerged.

Dodge City reverts, out of necessity, to a vegetarian diet, while the memory of the meat produced by the Harmless Slaughterer grows in the minds of the populace, passed down through the generations in another fast montage, "to the point where," according to the film's narrator, "it could only be described as Manna from Heaven, so sweet and succulent that no latter-day flesh could ever do it justice."

●

THIS LATTER-DAY FLESH—once a few scraggly specimens have been culled from the nearby woods and domesticated by a cabal of desperate farmers—is stringy, tough, and gray. Worst of all, the adrenaline produced in its death throes— carried out in a cloud of meth by frantic slaughterers in the old slaughterhouse—is so sour that few Dodge City citizens can stomach it, ravenous though they surely are.

The people get to wishing the Harmless Slaughterer would return, which, in due time—this being a narrative film—he does. He strides back into Town, visibly aged though clad in the same black cloak and felt hat as before, and gets back to work.

Or he would have, if he'd deemed any of the animals worth slaughtering. But, clearly, he doesn't. "Not a single viable specimen in the lot," he says to the camera, speaking in what, if I'm not mistaken, is Branson's voice. "Vicious, dumb, half-feral," he concludes, more to himself than to the camera, staring at the muddy ground he's standing on.

Thus it comes to be that he spends his days lounging by the fountain in Sacrifice Square, whittling a stick, speaking to no one.

No one, that is, until three teenagers—two boys and a girl, cousins perhaps—creep out to where he sits and settle in beside him. For a moment, the silence continues. The tension in the Temple is heavy.

Then one of them, the girl, clears her throat and says, "Sir, we can't help but ask . . . what did you whisper to those animals all those years ago? To make them taste so good?"

The Harmless Slaughterer smiles and motions for her to draw close. High on the fearlessness of youth, she brushes her hair from her neck, breathes deeply, and presses her pierced ear to his mouth. In a closeup, he licks his lips and places them against the cartilage. Then we see his throat vibrate.

In a medium shot, he leans back as she falls dead with a relaxed, slightly lewd smile on her face. Entranced, unable to stop himself, one of the boys submits to the same fate, falling on top of her.

Then—this is clearly the climax of the film—the third boy leans in to listen to the Harmless Slaughterer's message, but, instead of falling over, he smiles, deviously, wipes his ears with his palms as if to cleanse them of grease or oil, and kneels on top of his dead friends or cousins.

For a moment, he prays. Then he begins to eat of their goat-lobstery flesh, tearing into their necks and bellies with his teeth and fingernails while the Harmless Slaughterer watches from above, neither perturbed nor impressed. The meat looks soft and supple, like slow-cooked pork, and I don't mind saying that I experience a pang of hunger, here in the Temple.

When he's eaten his fill, the boy looks at the camera, motioning it in for a closeup, and says, lips covered in blood, "And this is one of the innumerable ways in which I became Blut Branson, uniquely vested, as I am, with private knowledge of God's Will and the inner strength to utterly disobey it."

Then, with a wink, he leans in and whispers in the Harmless Slaughterer's ear. The film ends with the Harmless Slaughterer falling onto the pile of partially eaten bodies, while the boy who has now revealed himself as Blut Branson dons the Harmless Slaughterer's hat and cloak and walks into the distance, vanishing into the same Hungarian gloom the Harmless Slaughterer emerged from.

Mother Son Statue

NEXT COMES what appears to be a quieter, more intimate film, perhaps one made more quickly and on a lower budget, though I know better than to speculate on the particulars of Branson's notoriously secretive production process.

This one opens in a small hut—a hovel, I want to call it—in which a man and a woman are walking around, testily lamenting their childlessness. They argue back and forth about whose fault it is, but they agree that this is the fundamental problem. Perhaps, they speculate, it will even spell the end of their marriage.

The couple gets so livid, finally, that the man storms out, slamming the door and stomping through the wind and dead leaves outside, kicking cans and soggy paper bags—it's clearly trash day—until he finds himself in a dim and desolate park.

He circles the benches tentatively, like he's never been here before, though I'd assumed this Town was his home—an unfounded assumption, I see now, based on conventions set by filmmakers far less singular than Blut Branson. In other films, I think, the characters tend to be residents of the places we see them in, unless otherwise stated, but in Branson films, even if they all take place, to one degree or another, in the timeworn Dodge City of his youth, the characters may or may not have any familiarity with the surroundings they find themselves called upon to navigate.

When I climb out of my thoughts enough to become again cognizant of what's happening onscreen, the man is sitting next to another man on a bench, all the other benches empty around them. If I'm not mistaken, the other benches are bobbing in the wind, knocking together, while the two men in the foreground talk from a position of relative stability, perhaps only because they're weighing their bench down.

To be more accurate, the man from the film's earlier scenes goes on talking, while the other sits in silence, not even nodding his head. As the camera slowly zooms in—or the men on the bench slowly bob toward us—it becomes clear that not only is the second man mute and immobile, but he's also made of clay or china. A Golem, I think. A statue.

This thought makes me lean closer to the screen, as if that way I might catch what he says if he ever decides to speak. But the other man just goes on and on, in what may be the longest monologue in Branson's whole filmography. He lists his failures going back to high school, his stalled ambitions, the many roads not taken, the many projects begun and never completed, the many unforced compromises he's made with himself over the years, until the statue looks so bored, even if its expression hasn't changed, that I half-expect it to stand up and walk away.

●

INSTEAD, what happens is that the man creaks to his feet and, after a long, indecisive pause of the kind that now seems indicative of his character, grabs the statue under its arms and heaves it off the bench, dragging it through the rain and the leaves, the bags and the cans, all the way back to his hovel, whose door he kicks open before dumping the statue in a heap in the center of the main room's floor.

The film pauses for thirty seconds here, while the woman takes the statue in, staring at it in what amounts to a photograph of the three of them all equally statuesque, nobody moving.

●

THEN THE FILM ZOOMS forward in time. The statue has been put in the spare bedroom—the one set aside for the child they never had—and there it sits, on a wooden chair, staring at the zoo-themed wallpaper.

"Just until we decide what to do with it," they assure each other, and, by extension, us. The statue is thus both integrated and repressed in their household, there but not there, in limbo.

Here we see a few scenes of life going on supposedly as usual, but interspersed are far more interesting scenes in which he and she both, independently, poke their heads into the child's room to see how the statue's doing. They begin to sit beside it, sometimes even pulling up another chair from the kitchen table, reading or napping against the statue's shoulder on long afternoons or evenings when the other's away.

Soon, they're leaning into the statue's ear and whispering, lips to its clay or porcelain head, disburdening themselves—so it seems, since we can hear no more than a muffled hum—of their deepest secrets, everything they've decided, for better or worse, to keep from one another. All the hard truths that could perhaps have saved their marriage if only they'd shared them upfront.

●

EVENTUALLY, as all situations must, this one reaches a breaking point. "I think I caught that thing looking at me," the woman says, when the statue's presence has cast an undeniable pall over the already-gloomy household. She puts down the chopsticks with which she's been eating Giant Chinese and says, "We're gonna have to throw it out tomorrow. It turned creepy all of a sudden."

The man nods, seemingly agreeing with his wife's decision, though it's a bittersweet interlude as he unrolls a plastic trash bag and sets it beside the statue, which he apparently plans to drag outside in the morning since, as he informs her and us, "Tomorrow's trash day. Again."

This long night serves as the film's climax. Both he and she take turns visiting the statue, whispering to it, saying their goodbyes, each blaming the other for its imminent disposal. This looks to be all there is, until, just before dawn, the wife wanders, or sleepwalks, naked into the statue's room and settles onto its lap.

Here commences a silent sex scene, as the woman rocks back

and forth on the naked statue, mouth open. It's impossible to know whether the statue had a penis all along or grew one just now, Branson having carefully framed every shot to leave this to the imagination.

When she's done—or when the statue is, since it appears to be moving now as well—she climbs off and pads back to her bedroom.

●

CUTTING TO THE MORNING—early-dawn light fills the hovel —the statue is walking around while its parents, if this is the right term, are still asleep.

"The strange thing is," the statue says in Branson's voice, staring at the screen, its lips moving out of sync with the words, "I heard everything they said to me. All along, all those secrets they whispered in my ear. Things no parent has ever knowingly told a child. That's how I became what I am. Everything I drew on later in life, for all my films, I learned in that room, when my parents thought they were alone, saying what they would never have let themselves say if they'd thought anyone was listening. When she visited me last night, I decided that was as good a time as any to come to life, but really, I was alive all along. That was just the moment of my conception, if you know what I mean. She became, in that moment, both my mother and my wife, just as I became, in a sense, both my father and myself."

I can see people in the Temple around me nodding, so I nod, too. When I look back at the screen, the parents are standing shocked before the statue as it approaches the man with the plastic trash bag outstretched. "I'm about to kill him," the voiceover continues, narrating the statue's thoughts now, or Branson's thoughts while directing the scene. "I'm going to kill the father I never had and put him out front with the trash, and live happily ever after in domestic bliss with my mother-wife, as is my prerogative after these long years of silence."

He proceeds to do just this. He walks over to the motionless man, engulfs him in the trash bag, and heaves him across the floor and down the front steps, where, in the distance, we see the garbage truck approaching.

The very final image is of the statue—now clearly a Branson stand-in, if not Branson himself, in pancake makeup—striding back up the steps to the hovel and, after kissing the woman inside, closing the door with a wink.

The Pale Oaks

THE NEXT TIME I GET the sense I'm watching a new film, after hours of soporific blues and purples dripping across the screen, it involves a hillside covered in lifelike but zombified figures. "Living sculptures," as the narrator explains. They sway and twitch in the breeze, their eyes cloudy but not quite opaque. Some follow the camera, and some don't—perhaps these are farther along a dimming trajectory, the nature of which the film is surely about to examine.

Two more humanoid figures appear on the hillside, almost identical, except that one looks older than the other, and worse for wear. Each sports a blue jumpsuit with the letters B.B. stenciled over the breast pocket. "One set of initials stands for Blut Branson," says the narrator, "and the other stands for Blut's Brother. But which is which? This is the hermeneutic puzzle the film invites us to consider."

The two figures grin at the screen, like they, too, have just heard the narrator's declaration, and are either in on the joke or wondering the same thing. Perhaps, I think, they're hoping the audience will solve it for them. I pay closer attention once this possibility has occurred to me.

"Here," one B.B. says to the other, "are the first of them, my early work, in the year immediately following your departure."

"My departure?" asks the other B.B.

The first one winks and moves on, deeper into the grove of living statues, which shudder and lean in as they pass, as if desperate for human warmth. One of the B.B.'s—they look the same from behind—breathes on one of the statues' faces, causing it to swoon and shrink into itself.

The other hurries to catch up, as the film dissolves to a scene much later in the day, the two of them reclining in a grove beside a weeping willow, a white gazebo visible in the distance. Wine bottles are scattered among salami rinds and heels of bread as they lounge, eyes almost closed, and the narrator speaks in what is perhaps an approximation of how their two voices might sound if conjoined in a single body.

"Years ago," this voice explains, "Dodge City underwent a Plague. It swept into Town from the Desert, and infected every man, woman, and child. The whole population at that time. Everyone, that is, except me. Why didn't it infect me? Well, on the day it arrived, I happened to be playing up at the Pale Oaks, the retirement community that had been built only a few years earlier, and was awaiting the first eligible Dodge City Retirees. We were, at that time, in a lull wherein all the former retirees had died, and no member of the current workforce, though some were getting up there, was quite over the hill yet. So the Pale Oaks stood empty, and, as I was undergoing some turmoil at home with my brother in those days," here each B.B. looks at the other, "I spent a lot of time in its drafty, paint-smelling corridors, which, though brand new, already felt haunted, perhaps with anticipation of their inhabitants rather than, as is more often the case, with their memory."

Here the two B.B.'s get up, clean their picnic mess, and walk into the dusk, past more of the living statues.

"Anyway," the voice continues, "once the Plague had thoroughly ravaged Dodge City, I put on some netting from the beekeeping room at the Pale Oaks, and went back to Town, among the Dead. Or the almost-Dead, I should say, since some of them were still twitching when I arrived. I loaded them onto a cart and dragged them up the hill, past the main buildings, and onto the sloping grounds of the Pale Oaks, where I'm walking now, with my wayward brother, who, I should say, was nowhere to be found during this transformative period. Let me tell you, the bodies were piled sky high. He must have fled Town, pursuing his own dark agenda, until that is . . ."

Here, one B.B. looks at the other, and they both smile conspiratorially. I take this to mean that they share a secret they're keeping from the audience.

The two B.B.'s walk into a dense cluster of living statues, which are now posed in what looks like a model of Sacrifice Square, the Hotel and the Temple recognizable behind it. "So, I dragged them all up here," the narrator continues, "including our parents, including our elementary school teachers, including our first three girlfriends, and I started to process them in the garage. Their corpses, that is."

The narrator clears his throat. "Now, I can't tell you exactly what the processing entailed, since that's a proprietary secret of the development company that built the Pale Oaks, even though they're obviously all dead, too, but what I can say is, er . . . well, look around. It wasn't an especially difficult task. It's just that no one else was up to it."

Here again, both B.B.'s make a gesture that encompasses the entire surrounding vista, which, once the camera zooms out, looks so much like Dodge City that I assume Branson shot it on the same set where he shot his other Dodge City films. The living statues shuffle in place, leaning toward one another and pantomiming conversation.

"After enough time, my brother, who thought he'd escaped us all to forge his own Life in the Desert, or in whatever sham-L.A. he assumed, with all the impudence of youth, lay beyond, returned, coughing, wheezing, bleeding from the eyes. Clearly, the Plague, all those years ago, had not spared him. It'd merely lain dormant in his system throughout his youth and early middle age, blooming up after a hard divorce and a . . . well, that doesn't matter. In short, he came back here, to the Pale Oaks, to be processed like all the others. Isn't that right?" Both B.B.'s look at each other. "To be turned into a living statue and posed in my Dodge City before it was too late."

The two B.B.'s enter what appears to be the Processing Room. A grinding and clanking overwhelms the Temple as the shot lingers on the locked doors.

●

THEN, one B.B. drags the other—now a living statue—back onto the lawn, and poses him at a picnic table with an older man and woman, behind a plaque that reads *Typical Dodge City Picnic Tableau (Property of The Dodge City Art World)*.

"Never mind all that about the Plague my brother told you," the narrator resumes, in a voice that is now clearly Branson's. "That's just a story that entered his head when I made him. A byproduct of the chemical fumes. What really happened is that I created all these people from scratch, up here at the Pale Oaks. I found a way—never mind how—to breathe life into the statues I was building in my workshop. I made a model of the Town I'd always dreamed of as a child, and then built all the people I saw in the dream and made them real, or at least real enough, and called the place where I posed them *Dodge City*. I brought them all to life, ending with my brother, who, in the dream, had left the Town we both grew up in. I wanted him back, and now, I've got him."

This B.B. walks proudly away from the family tableau, while the other remains, pouring tea from a Thermos. Shrouded by the dusk that's fallen over the Pale Oaks, he begins covering the living statues with tarps, tying them with bungee cords, and waving to the camera to stop following him, which, as the credits roll, it finally does.

SOMETIME AFTER THIS, the lights come up, and we rise, staggering, to our feet. Popcorn kernels and Jujubes fall from my lap as I take Big Pharmakos' hand and let him guide me back through the Lobby, past the posters for the films we've just seen, and out into the harsh light of Sacrifice Square, where it appears to be noon.

As we return in silence to wherever we live, I have a vision of us as survivors of an elevator malfunction or mine collapse, some long, dark ordeal in which we were all trapped inside together, and about which we will never speak again, though it has, in large part, made us who we are.

PHASE IV:

The Eternal Return

of Blut Branson

The Summoning Party

WHEN WE'VE RECOVERED from the Branson Retrospective, I learn that DCTV is preparing a set of Special-Edition DVDs of Branson's work, "to make available for the first time at home what, since time immemorial, has been available only in the Temple," as Dalton's televised speech puts it.

The not-so-secret underpinning of this shamelessly blasphemous event is that the Townspeople are all hoping it will trigger the reemergence of Blut Branson himself, who's been in reclusion so long by this point that some of us—though we'd never admit it—are starting to fear that he's disappeared permanently, once again.

Though it's an executable offense to presume to influence Branson's schedule in any manner, and thus referring to the DVD Release Party as a "Summoning Party" is a rarefied form of Suicide, it's what we're all thinking. C'mon Blut, we're all thinking. Come back already.

●

AFTER A MONTH OF WAITING, the day of the Release Party arrives. What's more, two of his most celebrated shorts have been included as special features on one of the DVDs—*2 Old Ppl*, about two best friends who, upon growing old, discover that one of them has turned into two old people while the other has turned into none; and *Our Beloved Carefree Child Was Murdered*, about a man whose profession it is to accept responsibility for having murdered teenagers who actually committed Suicide, so their parents don't feel guilty about not having done more while they still could.

In advance of the Party, all of downtown Dodge City is converted into an Anything-Goes Zone. For the past few days, Professor Dalton has been sitting on a folding chair in Sacrifice Square with a DO NOT DISTURB tattoo on his chest, getting his thoughts in order behind his beak mask, occasionally pacing around like a boxer, feinting and jabbing as he rehearses his speech.

●

THEN, because we can't wait any longer, the Release Party begins. We're tearing half-naked through the streets, eating fresh-killed hocks of goat and lamb, crushing boxes of wine against our lips and lapping it off one another, bellowing at the smoggy sky as the DVD truck pulls in. We hurl ourselves upon it, tearing open the back doors before it's stopped moving, rubbing our faces with DVDs, trying to watch them with our naked eyes.

We're buried in boxes, writhing in glory, heedless of suffocation. We go on like this until a slimy bursting overrides our glee, and we fall silent. Hundreds of Repressed Babies tear through the women among us. They rise from their mothers' shoulders, armpits, necks, and scalps, crawling out of the afterbirth to push aside DVDs and howl at the lights of Dodge City, the first they've ever seen.

As Big Pharmakos told me at the Bar once, many years ago Dalton pioneered a non-abortive family planning technique whereby fertilized embryos could be shifted out of the mother's womb and into another part of her body—the shoulder, the armpit, the neck, the scalp—and sit there, inert as benign tumors, until such time as the mother was ready to birth them, when the embryo would simply be pushed back into the womb with a pool cue and allowed to develop there as normal.

Though the arrival of Blanche Brine Daly added a competing method to the market, Dodge City women have apparently continued availing themselves of Dalton's treatment in large numbers, without incident until now.

Now, it appears, the absurd excitement surrounding Branson's DVD Release Party has caused the embryos to develop and hatch all at once, exploding from the places they'd been stored, emerging fully-formed from the wreckage of their mothers. I'm no expert, but they look larger than newborns should: more like two-year-olds, standing upright and bellow-ing to announce their belated arrival.

●

AS WE STRUGGLE to extricate ourselves from the mess, the Assistant Director, who occasionally intercedes in Town on Branson's behalf, appears with his camera out and ready, barking: "Test them for the Fear of Death! Test them for the Fear of Death!"

He's shooting frantically with a full crew behind him, people I've never seen before, and I start to wonder how much of this has been preordained for the sake of Branson's next film, and how elated I ought to feel if it has been, given that I'm here to witness it, perhaps even to partake. The chaos is such that no one can assess whether this is the Second Coming we've been waiting for, or a disaster spelling the End of Dodge City as We Know It.

The things we long for most, I think, unsure if I'm quoting a classic line or making one up, tend to arrive when we are least prepared to recognize them.

The Assistant Director's everywhere at once, swirling among the newborns, attaching mics to their bare chests. Then he turns to us and says, "Your job is to rank how scared of Death these newborns are. On a scale of one to ten."

No one moves.

"Now!" he shouts. "Do you want to be part of the next Bran-son film or not?"

Still no one moves.

"How are we supposed to find out?" someone finally asks.

"Ask them!!" the Assistant Director shrieks. "How do you think? Look at that pile of corrupted flesh. . . . That is their mothers. Show them that. Say, 'One day that will be you. What do you think about that? How does that make you feel?'"

Aware that my chance to have a hand in a Branson film is now or never, I run up to the nearest newborn and ask it these exact words. It doesn't respond. I try the next one, and likewise get no response.

"What if we get no response?" someone asks, sparing me the indignity.

The Assistant Director pauses, checking his rage before replying. "Speechlessness is a ten. Highest possible Fear of Death. They're all tens! They're all tens, aren't they!" he shouts, leaping up and down on the DVDs, indifferent to the Master's old work, focused entirely on the new. "Perfect! *Speechless upon the Altar of Death*! That's the title of Branson's next film!!"

The Hanging of Paul Broth
& The Dodge City
David Cronenberg

THE GLUT OF NEWBORNS FOLLOWING the arrival of the DVD truck sends Paul Broth straight back to the live oak he hangs himself from once a year, on the far edge of Dead Sir, the swamp in which all we've chosen to forget is submerged.

The original myth, as I've received it from Big Pharmakos, is that Paul Broth founded Dodge City as a community of Deserters from the Civil War and hanged himself when the Creeping Despair—at large in the country during those dark days—finally caught up with him. He remained suspended until the oak's branch broke, and he fell back into Dead Sir, on the Outskirts of what was by then a semi-functional, if dangerously isolated, Desert community.

Nowadays, he's known only for the periodicity of his going up into and coming back down from the tree, neither state a permanent antidote to the other. There's some debate as to whether he dies and returns from the Dead each time, or if he's found a means of hanging by his neck without switching all the way off. Either way, the observable fact is that he takes to the tree and depends from it once a year, coming down a few months later to resume his private life in the depths of Dead Sir.

Over the course of the months he spends hanging, Paul Broth makes a series of pronouncements about Dodge City, ever more finely delineating its innermost nature, revising our laws, our history, and our religion in a stream-of-consciousness that a rotating crew of Stenographers remains on hand to record, until the branch breaks.

●

EACH TIME HE RISES from the swamp, a procession that includes the Executioner and a select group of witnesses follows
him to the live oak. This year, the procession includes three of
the newborns who've occasioned Broth's premature resur-
gence; as well as Big Pharmakos; the Executioner, dressed in
his familiar jester costume, who has nothing to do but hold the
rope until Broth is ready; and me.

When we reach the live oak, we stand back, reminding ourselves that Broth's hanging is a natural phenomenon, no
stranger than the reopening of a century plant or the return of
an errant bird population after a winter away. He takes the
rope from the Executioner and climbs with it already around
his neck, creeping out onto the branch that has grown in place
of the branch that broke after he hanged himself from it last
year. This is the most precarious moment, as he's still mortal,
subject to the normal laws of physics: if he falls without the
rope to catch him, he could easily break a leg.

I can't watch. I close my eyes and think, If only I could climb
that high, maybe I could hang myself with impunity, too. The
question of which hanging is more canonical—that of Blut
Branson in the Hotel during The Dodge City Film Festival, or
that of Paul Broth here in the Outskirts—is, unsurprisingly,
the source of another Schism. One side argues that there could
never have been a Dodge City Film Festival if Paul Broth
hadn't founded Dodge City a century earlier, while the other,
more mystical side argues that there could be no ground in
which to dig The Dodge City Foundation, from which all trees
grow, had Blut Branson not dreamed it up first.

And, needless to say, there's a third side that argues that the
two hangings are versions of the same ineffable and indivisible
event, and that to speak of them using the language of either/
or is to do a great disservice to that which we, as mortals, were
made simply to venerate in all its inexplicable unity.

●

I DON'T OPEN MY EYES until I hear the twang of the rope breaking the body's fall. I'm no longer certain whether it's Paul Broth or Blut Branson and, for the moment, I don't care. Whoever he is, he hangs with his hands in his pockets, gagging, kicking his feet.

When he's recovered from the shock and entered whatever state of equilibrium he enters in this moment every year, he looks down at the newborns and speaks, his voice shredded like one of those anti-smoking spokespeople with the boxes in their throat. "There are several of you down there, I know. But, to me, there is only one. One of me up here, one of you down there. All things being equal.

"Yours is to be a grave and momentous fate," he continues. "A life's work that very few in this Town, or in any Town, even any city, any country, will come anywhere close to realizing. Since it is well known that the original Cronenberg has recently committed Career Suicide, I hereby dub you 'The Dodge City David Cronenberg.' The entire filmography of that august world figure is hereby commuted onto you, as a birthright. Whatever else you may do in the years ahead, in all the time you still have, it will be in excess of the vast accomplishment already behind you."

He gags, kicking his legs, spittle running away from his chin like a strand of wet dental floss, urine or semen staining his inner pantleg.

"To think of having made all the films of David Cronenberg at three days old"—They're only one day old, I think, though the parsing of one into three hardly comes as a surprise at this point—"the mind simply boggles." With this, he coughs and goes silent. He hangs like an actual hanged man, and we turn away fearing that, perhaps this time, he is.

This freights his pronouncement with considerable gravity. Though there's no consensus as to which newborn he anointed—assuming we are incapable of seeing all three as one—the fact that The Dodge City David Cronenberg is now among us, crawling at our feet, is no small thing. The significance of having fleshed out that body of work at so young an age, with so little self-awareness and next to no resources, makes us feel we are in the presence of a saint. The earlier ritual, conducted by Dalton for FEMA's benefit, seems even paler by comparison. This, we think, is at last the Real Thing. We vow to disregard the Annex Cronenberg who's already been anointed, remaking *Videodrome* in perpetuity. A False Prophet, we decide. A pox upon this land.

If the boy is a saint, though, he is one with an awful burden on his shoulders, a lifetime of asking himself, 'Where, after having created the life's work of David Cronenberg in three days, do I go in the years and decades to come?'

Obeisance to Blut Branson's Hundreds of Boyhood Homes and Thousands of Graves

A S WE SKIRT the edges of Dead Sir on our way back to Dodge City, three official Stenographers hurry to take our places at the foot of the tree, where, for the time being, Paul Broth hangs silent.

We make our way to the Welcome Center, where there's a buffet breakfast in honor of the event, all the pancakes served on paper plates printed with Paul Broth's face, the syrup dispensed from pitchers in the shape of his head. A life-sized plastic hanging tree stands in the center of the concourse, its branches ever full of crawling children, their parents stuffing down pancakes with one eye on the kids, ready to pounce the moment they crawl too close to the noose.

●

ONCE WE'RE FED, we process to the Street Where Blut Branson Grew Up, to pay our yearly obeisance to the Great Man's Boyhood Home, allowing the blurry distinction between Paul Broth and Blut Branson to disappear altogether.

We walk to the front door and knock, waiting for an elderly woman who appears as though she's sat there in silence all year, ready to open it and motion us in on this day of all days.

Inside, she begins, in a creaky, precise voice, like a recording, to show us the room where the Infant Blut was conceived and subsequently born, the room where his first crib stood until he was big enough to move into his Boyhood Bedroom, the basement where he sketched storyboards for his very first film, and the backyard where, the guide insists, he was greeted at puberty one starless night by an angelic or demonic visitor from another realm and given the Calling that would occupy the rest of his life, and by extension, the rest of ours.

●

WHEN THE TOUR IS OVER, we are let out back onto the street. Here, the procession disperses. Some of us turn left and others right, all in search of Blut Branson's Boyhood Home, of which there are hundreds, if not thousands, distributed all up and down this street, stretching past both horizons, though, of course, every guide is obliged to claim that there is only one.

I follow Big Pharmakos to a tremendous estate where we are informed that Branson grew up as the son of a mighty petroleum baron, fighting for self-definition under the shadow of soul-annihilating wealth. Next, we visit a lean-to overlooking a trash-choked creek, in which we're informed that Blut elevated himself from starvation-level poverty by shining shoes and scrounging fur from gutters, which he glued together to form shoddy fur coats, eventually saving enough to purchase his first camera, a second- or third-hand Polaroid with only two exposures left.

We enter the Boyhood Home in which Blut was one of seven babies born to the same teenage runaway, a former beauty queen from Tulsa; then we enter the Boyhood Home in which he was the only child born to a seamstress pushing fifty, a late-life miracle doted on to the point of suffocation by a mother who couldn't stand to be away from her pride and joy even long enough to let him defecate in private.

We pass the Wartime Blut Boyhood Redoubt, in which Blut's family, along with many others in Dodge City, sheltered during an unrecorded World War, a "World War 1.5, if you're going sequentially," the guide informs us, before we rush off to catch the Nomadic Home of the Tribe in which Blut's Carefree Prairie Boyhood was spent.

●

WE TAKE IN as many Boyhood Homes as we can, some of them Dodge City classics, the same every year, while others are brand-new, hastily erected, their specifics developed on the fly by guides who run the gamut from fundamentalists to charlatans. Then we stop for a quick lunch at Giant Chinese before visiting his thousands of graves.

PHASE V:

Kazakhstan

Location Scout

SUMMER APPEARS poised to unfold smoothly until The Dodge City David Cronenberg—in the end, one newborn was chosen at random among the three—shows up beheaded and disemboweled on an altar in Sacrifice Square with the words "there can be only One" carved into his chest.

A pall of fear and mourning comes over us, even as Dalton attempts to recast it as a Suicide and orders the remains buried in the Suicide Cemetery, between the oversized grave of the Cronenberg effigy and the miniature grave of the Boy Sparklehorse.

No one buys this. The more convincing theory, as explained to me by Big Pharmakos at the Bar last night, is that "Branson's getting jealous. Wherever he is, whatever he's up to, expect production on a new film to start up soon. He knows he can't afford to stay in the shadows much longer. Not if he wants to keep ruling this Town. Paul Broth has goaded him out of remission, deliberately choosing a New Cronenberg as a threat to Branson's stranglehold on our dreamlives."

●

AND, indeed, an announcement soon appears on The Dodge City Private Internet to the effect that Branson is seeking Location Scouts for his newest project and that "all interested parties, provided they are both trustworthy and courageous, should apply."

The time, I decide, is now or never. I've absorbed all I can from passive spectatorship and private study. I am, as they say, as ready as I'll ever be.

So, whether or not I meet the posted criteria, I put myself forward as an "all-around film assistant with razor-sharp instincts, if not exactly rock-solid skills," and modestly set my minimum desired salary at $15/hour. "All I really want," I type before deleting it, "is to get one step closer to the Man Himself. This is my humble desire."

●

AMAZINGLY, one of Branson's assistants calls me the next afternoon, waking me from my 3:05-3:15 nap. "Can you come by?" she asks, like I ought to know where she means.

"Sure," I reply, like I do. She hangs up without telling me when. I lie still until my alarm goes off at 3:15. Then I get dressed and head down to the Front Desk. Like a German tourist, I ask where Blut Branson's headquarters are located. Taking obvious relish in being asked, the Concierge unfolds the Local Attractions map and draws a tight circle at the outer edge of the official Walking Tour path. She reminds me to bring sunscreen and plenty of water, like I really am a German tourist and not someone who's lived in this Hotel for almost five years. To be fair, I don't know who she is, either, but I can't help feeling it's more her job to recognize me than it is my job to recognize her, even though, I allow, there are expo-nentially more faces on her radar than there are on mine.

When I get over this, I take her map and set out. After a hot, disoriented wandering spell, I arrive at what the map calls '*A complex of refurbished hostels, originally built by Paul Broth and his courageous band of Civil War Deserters, as a futile bulwark against the Creeping Despair.*'

●

THE PREMISES ARE SURROUNDED by a wrought-iron fence supporting a sign that reads *Branson Entertainments: Grindhouse and Arthouse* in rusted metal letters, clearly in homage to Lars von Trier's Zentropa Entertainments on the edge of Copenha-gen, unless, as ever, the line of influence goes in the other di-rection.

I'm considering rattling the gate to announce my arrival when an assistant rolls up on a golf cart, opening the gate from inside with a mobile device and gesturing for me to climb aboard.

"You got the call?" she asks, in a voice that might be the same as the one that called me. I nod and climb onto the cart beside her as she puts it in drive, taking us straight into the heart of the complex, which contains five large buildings and a number of smaller ones, like sheds, in clusters around the periphery. I can't believe I've lived in Dodge City this long without ever coming out here.

"Okay, get off," she says, jerking the cart to a halt. I tumble to my feet, dizzy, like I've just been on a plane, and follow her along a concrete path into the bunker. We pass through a thick plastic curtain and into a cement-smelling cavern, where the only lights on are red. I get the sense that unseen plant life is growing all around us.

I follow her further in, past tables laid out with guns and cash, into a side room with a door that requires a fingerprint scan to open.

●

INSIDE SIT AT LEAST FIFTY PEOPLE, applicants like me, I'm assuming, on plastic chairs under more of that harsh red light. At the focus of everyone's attention sits Branson himself—or the Assistant Director, playing Branson—in fatigues, combat boots, and a safari hat.

He turns and looks me over, calmly, and when he turns away, I have the feeling that he's seen all the way in. I take this as my cue to sit down.

"So," Branson begins, or continues, "as you all know, I have been incommunicado for the past while. I don't care to say where I've been. All that matters is that I'm now ready to get back to work. The next Blut Branson film is about to get underway. The real next film, not that Fear of Death footage we shot with the babies—that was just a trailer."

He leans to the side to reach into his back pocket and removes what looks like a plastic hood, which he unwraps and stretches over his head, sealing it around the neck. Then, stoic, though it doesn't look like he can breathe, he presses a button on his mobile phone and blinks somberly.

Gas hisses down from a sprinkler, and we all nod out.

●

WHEN I COME-TO, I'm in a glaring white room with six other people. We're laid on cots, tied up inside sleeping bags so tight we can only wriggle.

"The seven of you," says Branson's voice over an intercom, "have been selected as Location Scouts for my next film. The others have been let go. This is, needless to say, an immense honor. Your one shot at the big time. The jets leave for Kazakhstan in half an hour. Once aboard, each of you will receive a written description and a sketch of the location you are to find." He pauses to swallow whatever he's chewing.

"I have never in my life dreamed of a location for one of my films," he continues, his voice turning graver, "and failed to find it somewhere upon the Earth. What is in me is also out there. This is my brand, my claim to fame, my greatest asset."

I've seen this claim made before, in the first, most-cited interview in *Branson on Branson*. Its metaphysical hubris impressed me then, and impresses me even more now, to hear the man himself make it so boldly, with no hint that he's kidding.

"My chronic fear of flying has been well-documented for decades, so it should come as no surprise that I require your assistance in tracking these locations down." His voice keeps getting louder and slower. "Suffice it to say, if you find the location you have been tasked with finding, its inclusion in my body of work will serve as a source of pride for you for years to come. It will be your crowning achievement. You will not be credited outright, but you will know in your hearts, when you see my film, that the credit is yours."

As he's saying this, an assistant enters the room with a pair of scissors and, after asking each of us if we consent to execute the job we've been selected for, cuts us free. "Scout the area you're air-dropped into," says the assistant, "overlooking no corner of it, relentlessly seeking out the location described in the file you've been given. Your $15/hour will be paid upon your safe return, bearing photos of the location and its exact coordinates. You will be paid for twenty hours per day. Do not let Mr. Branson suspect that any of you has worked fewer."

Into the Steppe

I N A FEW MINUTES, I'm airborne, leaving Dodge City for the first time since I found myself briefly in Scotland with Big Pharmakos, en route to meet the Wicker Man. I can't see the other planes, but I picture us all taking off like an air-force squadron deployed to bomb a distant continent, Civil War Deserters finally ready to pay our patriotic dues. No, I think. Not to bomb that continent, but to pillage its natural resources, to dig them up and bring them back to Branson so that he might continue his career as a world-class visionary without ever leaving his bunker.

I look out the window at the landmass becoming a speck until the copilot rushes over and shuts the blind, saying, "Branson requires his Location Scouts to keep their minds clear until arrival at the designated site. Finding a Branson location is as much a matter of tuning one's inner landscape as it is of scanning the outer. May I suggest a sleep-mask?" He pulls it over my eyes as soon as the suggestion is made.

I BOB in darkness until the copilot, who's put on a "God Is My Copilot" T-shirt, returns to remove the sleep-mask and to inform me that we've touched down in Kazakhstan. I'd been expecting a concrete bunker airport on the outskirts of a ramshackle city, but it looks like we've landed on a dirt patch in the middle of the Steppe.

"Okay," he says, handing me a heavy backpack. "You're in charge from here. Read Branson's description of the location he's seeking, then walk in whatever direction you feel it lies. If you didn't have an innate sense for where that was, he wouldn't have chosen you. There's a phone in the pack that will ring when it's time for your pickup. You are to take pictures with that phone, as well. Food and water are also to be found in the pack. Ration them wisely."

Before I can ask anything else, he's back in the plane with the door locked. I can tell that pounding on it will only exhaust me, so I put my head down, shoulder the pack, and trudge into the grass. I adjust the pack's straps as I go, taking in the vastness of the landscape I'm about to get lost in.

●

FOR THE FIRST FEW HOURS, I walk through rocky fields and sparse vegetation, with nothing in mind except the location that Branson described in the file—*a lone tower in the midst of a rocky field, jutting into the sky.*

As it's getting dim on my first full day of walking, I pass an area demarcated by a sign that reads, in Russian and English: FIELD OF LANDMINES, PROCEED AT OWN RISK.

I proceed, training my eyes on my feet rather than on the horizon. For a while, I notice nothing out of the ordinary. Then, looking up to regain my bearings, I see what appears to be an art installation: a man arrested in the process of stepping on a landmine, his exploded body mixed with pieces of shrapnel, all of them hovering in midair, presumably supported by stakes or wires. Approaching, I think that one of three things must be true:

> 1) The landmine warning is a ruse for the sake of contextualizing this installation.
> 2) The dead man's real, but he's stepped on the lone landmine, and thus there's no further danger.
> 3) He's an example of what can still happen out here, and might soon happen again.

Though I try to console myself with vague musings about the unlimited reach of The Dodge City Art World, the fact that many more of these installations have begun to appear around me—all of them nearly identical, all men splayed apart by landmines, frozen in midair at the height of the explosions that killed them, if they were ever alive—doesn't bode well for the safety of this particular stretch of Steppe.

Soon, I'm so surrounded by hovering, exploded bodies that

the intense loneliness of the journey abates, much as I wish it would return. I fall to my knees, crawling through the sharp grass while peering at the spaces between my fingers, as if the most dangerous mines might be miniscule.

This goes on until I get so exhausted from crawling that I lie down and close my eyes right where I am, hoping the morning will dispel the funk that's come over me.

●

IT DOES, more or less. After some brisk walking at dawn, I pass another sign that reads NOW EXITING LANDMINE DISPLAY ZONE, which still doesn't resolve yesterday's art vs. reality dilemma, but does bring some relief. I walk on, without incident.

●

FINALLY, on what is by my count the third morning, I climb over a small hill and, on the other side, find exactly what I was afraid I might: the M-Tower, jutting into the sky. As soon as I lay eyes on it, a deep memory rushes to the surface.

The M-Tower, as I've called it since I was a child—due to the large stone **M** of its roof, which I always assumed stood for *me* or *mine*—is the structure I've gone to most frequently in my mind (perhaps this is what the M stands for, now that I think of it) when I needed to exit the circumstances around me and enter a place of pure cerebral calm. The running water inside the M-Tower is a self-renewing spring of fresh thought, where all my ideas have come from, where the dream of every Movie I've ever dreamed of making has been dreamt. I've spent whole days in here, drinking from the faucet on the top floor, looking out over a vast inner landscape absolutely identical to the one I'm standing in now.

Am I in my own mind? I wonder. Have I gone nowhere but deeper in? If not, how did Branson find this place inside me? What did he do to me while I was gassed?

Nothing feels more important than protecting the M-Tower

from Branson's influence. It's not his to steal, I think, my voice regressing to that of a child in my inner ear. But what's the alternative? Trudging on, into more grass, until my supplies run out? I imagine answering the phone when it rings and lying, telling Branson's people that there's nothing out here. Yelling at them for wasting my time. I reach in the pack and take out the phone, put it to my ear, and practice lying, but all that come out are gasps.

I've never been a good liar, not even in low-stakes circumstances. The thought of convincing an operation as militarized as Branson's of anything but the truth is more than I can fathom.

To keep from hyperventilating, I sit down and feel the M-Tower's shadow wash over me, cool as the sheets on my childhood bed.

It occurs to me that this is how Branson operates—each Location Scout he hires has an inner landscape of their own, which he unearths while we're under the gas. Then, he claims it as a product of his own imagination and sends us out to find it.

I try to follow the logic through: if I'm inside my own mind now, I think, what would it mean to emerge back into objective reality and lead Branson's people here? And after that, how would they film it and convey its essence to a mass audience inside the Temple? Are all the settings in all the Branson films I've ever seen stolen from the minds of others? Is this why they resonate so strongly in the Collective Dreamlife of Dodge City?

Perhaps his crew will make a scale replica and bring it back to Branson Entertainments. The thought of the actual M-Tower, here and real before me, being turned into a replica of itself and manhandled on a film set is too grotesque to dwell on. I spit to clear the thought, watching my dehydrated saliva trickle off the side of my shoe and into the Steppe.

Getting back to my feet, I creep around the bottom of the M-Tower, looking up at its majestic stone flanks, listening to the spring of pure thought flow through its piping, making my mouth water. It's clear that the only means of discovering what comes next is to seek it in there.

●

BOWING MY HEAD in reverence, I go in.

My Night in the M-Tower

INSIDE THE **M-TOWER**, I take my first gulp from the faucet and think, I'll spend the night alone in here, on the very top floor, surveying the landscape. If, in the morning, I still can't bear the thought of surrendering it to Branson, I'll prepare to take my last stand then.

●

WHEN I'VE EXHAUSTED MYSELF pacing the upper levels in contemplation, I either fall asleep and begin to dream, or fall into a waking trance in which my subconscious takes over all bodily and psychic function. Either way, I feel as though I'm finally seeing the M-Tower for what it is.

A shadow of its past or future self, I think, just like me. The synthesis rings true. One way or another, for better or worse, the M-Tower and I are inseparable. One expresses through architecture what the other expresses through biology and, maybe, a soul.

My perspective zooms out until I can see us both, one inside the other, a homunculus in a shell that in turn houses its own homunculus that in turn . . . There is something, though, that we can't see, neither the man in the Tower nor the Tower in the man. Some grander unity vanishes from sight as the sun goes down over the Kazakh Steppe, and the chirping of crickets and the dusty winging of bats fills the air.

If only, I think, the sun would rise in the morning over a slightly different world—or if a slightly different sun would rise— some fruition would surely be possible. Some means of seeing far enough inside myself, or all the way beyond myself, such that I would no longer waste my days and years in the half-hearted attempt to work for someone else, but would rather come at last fully into my own, and the embryos that have incubated for so long inside me would hatch, and the whole world would know what they are.

If I could only find the right window, I go on thinking, to gaze out from the M-Tower onto the astral landscape beyond, or else perhaps a hidden staircase within, a staircase that leads all the way down, to the vault or the altar or the catacombs, whatever it may be, to the foundation itself, then there, hidden, would be what I'm lacking: the knowledge, the insight, the stamina to force into reality—to hammer into the world—that which has lain latent and rotting for far too long in my gut, rendering me fit only to grovel at Branson's feet.

I'm pacing the Tower maniacally now, up and down its cold stone stairs like some undead caretaker, skidding in the dust and catching myself just before falling out the wide-open windows, the night deep and thick as I chase the deliverance that I feel certain is at hand, closer than it's ever been, and closer than it'll ever be again.

I decide that it's either a glimpse of my past—an answer, finally, to the question of where I came from—or else of my future, a long-delayed clue as to where, after all this circular travel, I'm going or ought to go. I'd kill for either one, I think, for any certainty at all, any clue even, any means out from under the shadow of Blut Branson and into my own skin, the skin of a grown man, a real Director, someone capable of . . .

●

I COLLAPSE on one of the stone staircases, and wake up, if I'd been sleeping, or fall asleep, if I'd been awake. Either way, the feed is cut. The scene is over.

My last, awful thought, just before total darkness envelopes me: might it be possible that all of this, every thought I've just had, is nothing but a canned version of yet another Blut Branson Origin Story, one more, among so many thousands, of how the Great Man came to be, and why his Greatness—as if I didn't know already—so infinitely outstrips my own?

●

I WAKE UP on the stairs, my back sore, my mouth dry, and my only thought is, Whatever I saw last night, in the depths of my delirium, I need to see it again. I didn't get a good-enough look the first time.

I sit, wincing, and pledge—though there are no witnesses—to build a version of the M-Tower in Dodge City, so that I might visit its secret-filled inner chamber on a daily basis, as often as necessary to find what I know is hidden there.

Somehow, I think, with a little luck and a lot of work, the truth about me will not remain buried forever. Yawning, I hear myself say, "My M-Tower isn't yours to take, Blut Branson. Unless you kill me, I'll find a way to rebuild it."

As soon as these words escape my mouth, Branson's agents parachute down and gag me with an ether rag.

Dead Ringers 2

THE NEXT TIME I WAKE UP, I'm in a bed that's actually pretty comfy, with a blanket pulled up to my chin and, though I don't reach my hands up to check, a tightness that feels like a sleeping cap on my head.

In front of me is a combined TV/VCR unit in a wall-mounted frame, with an empty VHS box on top. The box says *Dead Ringers 2: A David Cronenberg Film*, though I have the sense that this is merely its title and that it is, like all films perhaps, in reality a Blut Branson film.

Still, I fall right in, as I always do with Cronenberg films, even apocryphal ones. This one involves the same twin duo from the original, again played by Jeremy Irons, though by this point he looks well on his way to aging into a poor man's Jeremy Irons.

In this scenario, the twins are film professors at a shoddy rural college, sort of a Miskatonic University vibe; it's maybe even shot on the same set as *Re-Animator*, now that I look closer. The professors teach a Monsters of the Korean New Wave course, though all the clips they screen are blacked out—probably, I think, because Branson couldn't secure the rights. So, we see the students reacting in awe to what we know is nothing.

As in the first *Dead Ringers*, the twins make sure that only one of them is ever seen at a time, so as not to let on that they aren't the same person. Their angle—one that has aged poorly, I note—is to sleep with as many students as possible, same as in the original. Here I begin to wonder, unless it's just the ether talking, if perhaps this *is* the original, questioning my memory of that 1988 film taking place in a gynecology clinic in Toronto.

The heart of the drama, once the film has established its premise and reached the point where this is no longer enough to keep the viewer viewing, centers on the problem of one twin growing more infatuated with a certain student than the other twin wants him to be, and by extension less infatuated with his twin than their symbiosis requires.

In this case, it's a goth girl with a very conspicuous nerve disease. Like the worst case of shingles ever contracted, her nerves have grown outside her body and are hanging down her face like a mane of dreadlocks. I picture her being played by Rob Zombie's wife, Sheri Moon Zombie, but even in my semi-delirium, I'm fairly certain this isn't the case. A poor woman's Sheri Moon, I think.

One twin wants nothing to do with her, but the other, either locating a genuine fetish in himself alone, or simply eager to torment his twin by acting on a non-shared desire, tries to seduce her anyway.

This plays out in a quickly dashed-off "office hours" montage, at the end of which they go back to the bungalow that he, Elliot (the names, too, are reprised from *Dead Ringers 1*) shares with his more sensitive, self-protective twin, Beverly.

While Beverly sleeps in the spare bedroom they call *the Nursery*, Elliot has sex with the goth girl—whose name, he learns, is Chloë, a double-major in film theory and Japanese—in the tub.

●

SHE LEAVES in the morning, and Elliot struts into the breakfast nook, ostensibly to gloat to Beverly, but before he gets the chance, we see that his face is riven with wormlike, protruding nerves, his lips crawling, bloody fluid dribbling from his nose into his mouth.

Beverly butters his toast with a derisive *I told you so* smile as his twin writhes. Soon, Elliot's nothing but a rubber-band ball of exposed nerves, tangled in himself, shrinking. Even his voice is swallowed up.

●

I DRIFT OFF at this point in the video, waking to find Elliot shrunken to the size of a child, Beverly now in the position of caring for him, as if this new entity were his son, not his twin.

Chloë is back in the picture, as well, living with Beverly as a sort of mother to the baby-Elliot, as if he were the natural offspring of their night together in the tub. It's not clear whether she understands that the man she's living with isn't the same as the man she slept with—perhaps their formerly perfect twindom had her fooled more than anyone, though she must know she hasn't given birth.

I get the sense, from watching Beverly's performance in these scenes, that he's jealous of his shrunken twin, wishing that he could've been the one to regress and to be cared for instead. "Even a horrible nerve disease like that," I imagine him thinking, in voiceover, "would be worth it if I could have back all the years I've wasted in the process of becoming whatever I am now . . . a sundered twin . . . an unwitting father . . . a rural film professor doomed to irrelevance."

I can't help hearing Cronenberg himself, now that he's committed Career Suicide, likewise wishing he could have back the gory, sleazy years of his youth. "If I could just get myself back to the 80s," I think, pretending to be him, "and make *Videodrome* and *The Fly* and *Dead Ringers* again . . . just one more time, I'd . . . I'd . . . I'd . . ." I nod off wondering what I'd do if I were Cronenberg, granted permission to return to the 80s for one day only.

●

WHEN I WAKE UP, Blut Branson's leaning over me with a scalpel in one hand, shining a laser in my eye with the other.

This dislodges a new, frightening supposition, just as the tape auto-rewinds in the VCR: what if I've been shown this video as a form of infantilization, before my reckoning with Blut begins . . . a sort of video-anesthesia . . . a forced regression to my own helpless infancy, same as the twin onscreen. . . .

As he scours my face with the laser, the phrase that keeps

moving through my mind is softening me up . . . softening me up . . . he's doing all this to soften me up.

I'm still repeating this phrase as he focuses the laser behind my ear and makes the first incision. It doesn't hurt. I know I should be grateful, but all I can access is terror when I realize the pain isn't getting through.

Perhaps, somewhere in the course of watching the film, my nerves were likewise pulled out of my body, I think, aware that the scalpel is inside my skull now, probably erasing my memory of this whole episode, uprooting the M-Tower so thoroughly I won't even know that it's gone.

PHASE VI:

The Fetus

Shantytown

A Ghostly Broadcast

NEXT THING I KNOW, I'm back in my Room, slack-jawed before my laptop, a swatch of gauze taped to my throat. Have I had a lobotomy? I sense this is a question—perhaps even *the* question—that my current mental state will prevent me from being able to answer. To take my mind off it, I plunge into archival Branson research on The Dodge City Private Internet.

"It's well known among those who follow the Lives of the Great Directors that, from 1991 to 1996, Blut Branson was dead," I read. Though the whereabouts of his body were unknown during those years, no one, not even Big Pharmakos, was optimistic or superstitious enough to consider him still-living. All anyone ever told me—I remember discussing this episode with a few locals at the Bar sometime earlier this year—was that one day Branson committed "a very private form of Suicide," echoing David Lynch with the lament that, "Movies aren't really my bag these days," and booking himself into The Dodge City Private Crypt.

I'll admit that I've had a similar thought on occasion, what with today's seemingly infinite, and infinitely disposable, online content streams competing for our diminishing attention . . . swallowing the remnants of what used to be the Sacred Art of Cinema with barely a belch . . . and . . .

I click onto a new page and read about how the set of the film Branson was working on when he died became a paralyzed village on the Outskirts of Dodge City, "an Annex of the Annex." The cast and crew took to hanging around, eating craft services until they ran out and then beginning to eat one another, waiting for instructions, refusing to accept their project's demise.

●

I PRESS PLAY on an audio file embedded in a new webpage and am immediately sucked into a broadcast, dated May 27,

1991. After a few seconds of crackle, I hear Branson answering questions posed to him by what sounds like a young Professor Dalton. Since this same page claims that Branson died on May 28, 1991, I can't help but pay attention.

The broadcast is structured like a call-in radio show, where Dalton keeps stopping to announce the phone number, soliciting "those burning questions you've always had for Blut, but never found the courage to ask."

Various people call in to ask, "Where do you get your ideas?" and "Which B.B. were you in *The Pale Oaks*?" One woman wants to know if thirty-five is too late to embark upon a film career ("You're still a baby!" enthuses Branson, his tone unusually warm).

Then I hear my own voice come on the air. I increase the volume on my laptop. "What about your unrealized *Zoos of the Infinite Blue Horror Hole* script? Any chance of that seeing the light of day?" I hear myself ask.

"Well," Branson begins, as Dalton coughs politely in the background, perhaps aware that we're straying into uncomfortable territory, "now that you mention it, I have been thinking that maybe . . ."

Thus begins a long, frightening discussion of Branson's great unrealized project. "The idea," Branson explains, on the eve of his demise, "is to consider an infinite recurrence of zoos: endless sets of higher, or supposedly higher, species watching the behavior of lower species, while one of them is imprisoned and the other is free. Each zoo spectator is the zoo animal for the next-higher species, so that each is at once knowing subject and unknowing object . . . but what's interesting to me is the idea that it's not the behavior of any given species that entertains the next higher species (and by extension the film's eventual viewer, were it ever to be made), but rather the attention that each species pays to the lower species . . . the *mode* of attention, if you will, the specific qualities of it, the nature of each species' prurience and perversion when it comes to the lives of those less fortunate. . . . Do you see?"

"Yeah," I hear myself say, from all the way back in 1991, unless it's someone much older playing me, "like those State Prison photos that made such a splash in The Dodge City Art World?"

"Sure. Petra's paintings. I own several. Of course, stories where characters believe they're the zoo visitors only to discover that they're the zoo animals are a dime a dozen, but what sets my idea apart is its infinitude . . . how the pairs magnify out, across spacetime, to a dizzying level of complexity, as the creeping suspicion that there can never be an end of zoos begins to dawn on the viewer, who, while watching, may also come to feel watched."

I glance at my window, glad to find the shades drawn.

"The only problem," he continues, after a lengthy pause, "is that I don't yet have a suitable macro-narrative . . . nor any real characters to speak of. But the set, in the Desert just outside Dodge City, is built and ready to go."

"Then how will you work through the next phase?" I ask, my voice sharp and confrontational now. "Aren't you afraid your crew will mutiny if you don't keep them busy?"

"That," says Branson, "is the kind of question that can make a filmmaker disappear."

●

THE BROADCAST GOES DEAD as I scroll down the webpage, to where it says, "After coming back to life in 1996, Branson declared that all his previous projects had died with him, and that he was now a 'New Man, dedicated entirely to New Work.' Needless to say, there are those in Dodge City who interpreted this statement metaphorically, claiming that Branson had simply changed his outlook during his time away, and those who interpreted it literally, claiming that he was indeed a new man, an Imposter, and that the old Blut was either truly dead, or alive and well and simply biding his time in the hills. There is, as of this writing, no consensus as to which version is true."

I close my laptop and scribble notes in my journal: *Patchwork of childhood influences—all the fairytales I absorbed as a child were, for me, literally true inside the M-Tower, where I absorbed them—all my previous selves were trying to make me into what I needed to become in order to take Branson on, the minotaur in the labyrinth of my own influence . . . the giant between me and my becoming.*

Now I'm liberated, on the prowl, like a samurai who doesn't yet know his own power, or his own freedom to wield that power. . . . Somehow I need to create for myself an avatar within Branson's world, a better self to be as I explore his baroque imagination, the zoos within zoos of his refracting gaze. . . .

And thereby eviscerate him from the inside out, just as I did in 1991, but for good this time. . . . If I was capable of killing him once, I'm capable of killing him again.

●

I TAKE A MEZCAL from the minibar and walk out to the balcony, scratching my gauze. I look across Town, all the way to the lights of Branson Entertainments, and wonder if the set he abandoned when he supposedly died is still there, deep in the Desert.

Stuffing my journal into my backpack and finishing my drink, I decide to find out. As I ride the elevator down to the Lobby, I try to tally all the time I've wasted here—far more than five years, if it's true that I was calling into the radio station back in '91—and decide, as the elevator doors ding open, to finish the film he abandoned. Whether or not it's exactly what I've always imagined myself doing, it's what I'm going to do now. The true beginning of my Life in Movies. Whatever version of me spoke up in 1991 had the guts to goad the Great Man into Suicide, so surely now, all these years later, I ought to have the guts to pick up where he left off.

I Make My Way
to the Abandoned Set

HAVING RESOLVED to take my stand, I walk up the Strip to ULTRA MAX and buy a camcorder, a tripod, a set of wireless mics, and a memory stick. Then I come back to my Room, take a shower, throw all my supplies in a backpack, and head out again.

As I'm passing the Front Desk, I see the Concierge arguing with a man who, I gather, attempted Suicide by poison but was resuscitated after seventy-two hours. "I shouldn't be charged for that time!" he shouts. "Not full price, anyway! I didn't think I'd ever be in this position, so how can you expect me to have saved for it? I didn't even bring my wallet. That was the only kindness I showed myself!"

"Sir, as a Hotel, our business is to rent you a room, at a fixed rate per day," replies the implacable Concierge. "What you do in there is your business."

The man grows so livid he opens his mouth without producing any sound. The Concierge places a mint on his outstretched tongue. I nod, though she's not looking at me, and make my way out.

●

BY THE TIME I MAKE IT to the Outskirts, it's late dusk. I turn on my flashlight, sweeping the terrain for any sign of Branson's set. I pass former stores, car bodies without wheels and, twice, piles of dead dogs. For reasons I can't explain, I have the thought, on both occasions, that these sinister piles are concealing something even worse—that the mass of rotting dogflesh is more decoy than travesty. I don't explore this thought beyond filing it away for use in a possible future film.

And what of Branson's Kazakh film? Did my resistance in the M-Tower prevent its being made? Or is my lobotomy clouding my judgment, such that I'm now mistaking a premonition for a memory?

●

JUST AT THE POINT WHERE I DEBATE whether to turn back, maybe shoot some footage of those dead dogs and call it a day, a row of torchlights appears on the horizon, making me feel like a medieval exile, seeking succor in the territories. This idea excites me: perhaps, as a Director, this will be my niche. I'll show up at defunct sets along the road and, under guise of seeking shelter, take charge.

I'll be somewhere between a Mayor and a Director, I think, a Serial Rescuer of Dead Movies. Somewhere between Paul Broth, fleeing the Civil War to found a new Town in the Desert, and Blut Branson, warping that Town into his own private dreamscape. Though part of me fears, at this late date, that any aspiration to such a Life in Movies is no more than the half-formed dream of a much-younger man, I see no other path forward, and it's clear that the last chance to remain in my Room, awaiting the future, is now behind me. So, barring any Revelation, this will be the road I take.

●

I CROSS into the circle of torchlights, keeping my shoulders back and my chin up so that whoever's here doesn't pounce. All around me are plywood façades, half-finished buildings, marquees bearing two or three letters at most. Pickaxes piled in wheelbarrows. A miniature Dodge City where history never ran its course.

Folding tables laid out with bottles and cups fill all the blank spaces, Blut being rather infamous as a heavy on-set drinker. I pour myself a bourbon and Coke and walk with it in my hands, more as a prop than as a real drink, though I do take a few sips.

It's impossible to tell if the disrepair is due to the buildings never having been finished, or if they've degraded in the years since preproduction ceased. Either way, it's a shantytown now.

So, here I am, I think. In the Square I see nothing but children, and not very strong or healthy-looking ones, at that. They lurch around, falling to their knees every few steps, carrying plastic plates away from a fire where the biggest among them are doling out what looks like the meat of their weaker kin. The scene reminds me of the charity dinners the Quakers set up on summer Fridays in Sacrifice Square.

I approach the fire, figuring I'll ask for a plate and thereby ingratiate myself by breaking bread. But before I get there, a searing pain in my left ankle brings me down. I land on a piece of foam painted to look like a cobblestone, surrounded by tiny peering faces, not so much deformed as unformed. The one that bit me is now chewing a knob of my flesh.

The others simply open and close their mouths like they're breathing underwater. It takes a moment to see them for what they are, or were:

Fetuses.

They look almost like babies, but not. Their faces are—I make a note of this phrase in the verbatim section of my brain—*too innocent*. I immediately consider this as a possible title for my film.

As I sit with them, listening to their low, mournful chatter, I remember a story Big Pharmakos told me when we were very drunk one night early in my time in Dodge City:

"Not that long ago," he began, in the Lobby of the Hotel, which I did not yet know would be my residence for the next chapter of my life, "there was a scandal at the abortion clinic. After decades of protests, attacks, even a few murders, The Dodge City Pro-Life League came up with a far-more radical approach. Instead of killing the unwilling mothers or their doctors, who, after all, would simply be replaced with others just like them, these Pro-Lifers thought, Why not address the problem itself by reanimating the aborted fetuses?"

Here, sitting on the foam-cobblestones of the shantytown, I recognize my companions—my cast and crew, I think, a bit prematurely, perhaps—as the living embodiments of Big Pharmakos' story, which, at the time, I'd had more than a little trouble believing.

"Using a technology the nature of which no one understands," Big Pharmakos continued, "these Pro-Lifers snuck into the trash behind the clinic late one night, after a big sack of fetuses had been deposited, took them all out, brought them back to a lab somewhere and, well . . . as far as anyone knows, regrew them in tanks."

The strange thing about these fetuses, I think, studying those surrounding me more closely, is that they must have been given the chance to gestate for far longer than they would have had they remained in the womb. For them, there never came the point of "now it's time to make your way out"; they just grew on and on in their tanks, getting bigger without ever crossing the line between fetus and baby . . . and now, here they are, fending for themselves in a world they were never meant to inhabit.

It reminds me of that old *Unholy Family* episode, "The Dodge City Partial-Abortion Scheme." This, I think, is a version of that, as is Big Pharmakos' story, all approximations of the Truth, which remains out of reach, palpable in its general form but never its specific facets. Or vice versa, I think, suddenly unsure which way the saying goes.

"All Blut Branson films are but shards of a single divine Movie," I think, again uncertain whether I'm quoting or coining a phrase, as well as whether I'm deepening or changing the subject. I feel an inrush of both fear and relief to realize that I forgot to pack my copy of *Branson on Branson: The Master Speaks.*

Aware that I'm close to the point of having done enough thinking for one day, I yawn, close my eyes, and watch the rough framework of my film fall into place. If I can only get these fetuses to portray the children they never were and will never be, I think, limping toward the façade of the Hotel in search of a place to rest my ankle, there will be a built-in sense of drama, palpable beyond whatever ability I may or may not have as a Director.

"You were given a second lease on life," I imagine shouting at them, through a bullhorn, as the opening scene unfolds. "Are you glad? What use have you made of it so far, and what plans, if any, do you have for the future? Will you finally, after so many years of procrastination, manage to shuck off the mantle of Blut Branson and come into your own? Are you at last ready to take your stand as born beings?"

Return to Branson Mansion

Part II

BEYOND THE OUTSKIRTS of the shantytown—the façade of the Hotel proved to be only a façade, and thus
no place to rest—I make my way back into the Hollywood Hills and along Mulholland Drive to the clifftop where I now feel at least partly at home. I creep past the
underlit hedges, past the carriage house where the limo is
stabled, and into the mansion, which I now assume will be
empty.

●

SO FAR SO GOOD. I've explored all the rooms and found no
one inside. I help myself to a beer from the fridge—I don't dare
try any of the food, given that there's no way to estimate how
old it is—and settle into an armchair in the den to look over
my notes and ice my ankle.

Nodding off, I fall into a happy dream of waking in the morning to be driven down the hill by my chauffeur, all the way to
the set that I am now unilaterally in charge of, the Great Man
in his private sanctum, ready to call the shots.

Blut Branson Reemerges from The Dodge City Private Crypt

I'VE SPENT the past two months living in Branson Mansion, working on a script for what I hope will be the first of several films I'll make out here with the reanimated fetuses. They certainly seem up for it.

My script—I tried to recall *Regression Pills*, but, in memory, the concept seemed to belong more to Branson than to me, as did my notion of the fetuses playing the children they would never become—is about a trio of best friends who unwittingly hire a suicidal prostitute and then stage an elaborate funeral for her in the Suicide Cemetery, where they end up breaking their own hearts by pretending she was the long-lost love of their lives, reading out the eulogies they'd originally written for themselves, to be read by one another many years hence. It's overlong, full of digressions, but I'm proud that it is, if nothing else, a substantive piece of writing, my first since my entanglement with Branson Entertainments and probable lobotomy.

●

I'M ON SET, inventorying camera and sound equipment, trying to determine what we'll need before we start shooting, when a siren in the shantytown's model of Sacrifice Square brings all activity to a halt.

I turn to face it, as do the fetuses, their pickaxes resting on the cardboard cobblestones. A screen above the marquee of the Temple comes alive with a newsfeed so stylized that, at first, I think it's a short film.

I watch as Blut Branson emerges from The Dodge City Private Crypt for the *nth* time, dusting himself off and blinking through harsh sunlight. As *Unholy Family* reporters shove microphones in his face, he says, "Look, everyone, all I'll say is this: I, like Dante, had to go to hell for a while. Now I'm back, ready for my Late-Career Renaissance."

With that, he pushes past them, hurling a reporter out of his face with enough force to send the rest scurrying. As he marches out of frame, I become certain that he's coming straight for me.

●

FOR A LONG TIME AFTER HE'S GONE, the camera lingers on the façade of The Dodge City Private Crypt, a two-story stucco building somewhere in the Outskirts, its glass doors clacking in the breeze.

I first heard about the Private Crypt a few years ago, when there was a rash of desecrations of the graves of formerly luminous Directors, Branson's foremost among them. The question, as ever, centered on which deaths should be viewed as Suicides, and thus interred in the Suicide Cemetery, and which should be ascribed to natural causes, and thus abandoned to memory. As far as anyone knows, Branson's body was moved to the Crypt as a temporary solution until the nature of his own possible Suicide could be resolved, which, needless to say, it never was.

I've always thought of the Crypt as an even lower-brow Chelsea Hotel—a Chelsea Motel, catering to a dead rather than to a down-n-out clientele. Though I've never been inside, I've heard Big Pharmakos describe rows of rooms along a dingy tile hallway, doors shut but not locked, the Dead Luminaries of our Town posed like Tangier junkies on the nod.

It's not lost on me that I'm using the last of my time before Branson shows up to indulge these thoughts about the Private Crypt, which still appears silently onscreen, as if my inner monologue were the narration of the broadcast. I'm doing this instead of making any push to set my film in motion, so as to appear to have become a real Director in his absence. I feel like a teenager whose house party has spun out of control: I've just gotten word that my parents are on their way home, and there's no time to clean up, or even to detach whoever's still screwing in the laundry room.

●

I CAN FEEL MYSELF SWAYING, looking at nothing in particular, as the fetuses bustle around, dressing the set, plugging in cords and wires, testing mics, wheeling by racks of costumes, oblivious or indifferent to the fact that production's about to be shut down yet again. My script hangs by my side, dangling between my thumb and forefinger, which are sweating through the pages.

I'm still in this state when Branson snaps his fingers in front of my eyes. I open them and feel my script land on my foot. Slowly, almost robotically, he bends down, picks it up, and pages through it.

Then, we look at each other in earnest. I feel my lower back convulse. Something's wrong: it's Blut, but it's not Blut.

Up close, I see that he's grown a thin, white goatee, and his eyes are strikingly bluer than I remember. Minty, frosty blue. I can't say what shade I remember them being, but I can tell they're off. These are not Blut Branson's eyes. Are they those of the Assistant Director? Or was the man I always took to be Blut actually the Assistant Director, and now, at last, the Real Blut Branson is here?

"Hey," he says, looking up from my script to survey the shantytown. "What're you doing out here?"

"This is my set!" I want to yell in his face. "I'm directing my first Movie is what I'm doing out here!"

"Nothing," I say. "I just, uh . . ."

He nods. "Well, thank you for visiting. I have to get back to work now." Then he strides off among the fetuses, telling them what to build and criticizing what they've built already, checking my script every few seconds.

I know that if I don't start moving right now, I'm going to freeze in place. Then, at best, I'll thaw and trudge back to

Dodge City and chalk this whole venture up to experience, telling Big Pharmakos how we learn more from our failures than we do from our successes over ten or twelve beers at the Bar at noon.

I close my eyes and try to think. I think about gouging Branson in the head with a pickax and dragging him back to The Dodge City Private Crypt, telling the doorman, "This one wasn't ready for life on the outside."

●

BUT BY THE TIME I'VE THOUGHT this scenario through, Branson—or the Branson-lookalike—is already deep in rehearsal, reading aloud from my script like he wrote it, the fetuses gathered at his feet.

I suffer a moment of complete aloneness, overwhelmed by the extent of the Desert around me and how far from home, security, and any kind of legitimate employment I've allowed myself to drift.

●

THEN, something behind my forehead clicks: no, I think. It doesn't end this way.

I imagine leaving the shantytown behind and setting out into the Desert, convinced that if I march with enough purpose, at least a few fetuses will follow.

With my loyal troupe in the open Desert surrounding what's now the set of Blut Branson's new film—the first of his Late-Career Renaissance—I'll improvise a scenario of my own. It will be a counter-film, a film made in tandem with his, designed specifically to refute it, like those legends of deranged cinematographers sneaking in at night and shooting their own carnivalesque visions on the sets of the German Expressionist masterpieces.

A film about an Imposter, a simulacrum-Branson who returned from the Dead to hijack the career of his legitimate heir, just as surely as the undead David Cronenberg is said to have begun working through the avatar of his son, Brandon.

In a fugue of sudden confidence, I decide that, as well as writing and directing this film, I'm going to star in it. I'll stand before the fetuses with this resolve firm in my mind. However smothered it ends up making me feel, I'm going to become Blut Branson, the Real one. I'm going to plunge down until I find the thing in me that's the same as the thing in him, and then I'm going to bring it back to the surface and hold it up for all of Dodge City to behold.

"Unlike all of you," I'll declare to the fetuses, "my effort to be born will not end in vain. The Imposter-Branson who's forced his way into our midst is a blessing in disguise, my doorway to the Realm of Greatness. The Blut Branson we knew and loved is dead. Or was, for a long time. Now He's back. I am He. He is I. You are looking right at Him, and He will be your Director from now until we finish the work that it is finally time for us to begin."

The Passion of Blut Branson:

An Origin Story

J
UST BEFORE I EXECUTE in reality the escape I have so lavishly imagined, Blut Branson, or his proxy, creeps up behind me, puts a hand on my shoulder, and sits me down in the sand.

"Believe it or not," he begins, immediately inducing me to doubt whatever he plans to say, as well as his reasons for leaving the set to say it, "I was once a regular guy like you. Years before your time, decades really, Dodge City was a lot like it is now. They say nothing lasts forever, but there's an inertia to Towns like this that makes you wonder. In any case, all those years ago, I found myself hanging around, not doing much of anything. As I say, a lot like you."

I open my mouth, but he continues before I can speak.

"I had dreams, sure, but I was fairly certain they'd die inside me, unhatched like the slowly rotting eggs of a platypus. I saw no other fate for them. Thus, I felt no real guilt about letting mine go soft, like those of all the Bluts before me.

"But then something happened. As I believe is often the case with Great Men like myself, an event outside the purview of my Will provided the impetus that set me on my course. Or, more accurately, the true extent of my Will first manifested from a source outside my body.

"A great Melancholy came over Dodge City. Over the course of one summer—this must have been 1976 or '77, as I remember ber Cronenberg's *Rabid* making waves with my few semi-intelligent friends—all of our small, private melancholies merged. Through a crack in the Dreamspace, or perhaps in the actual sky, the idea began to overwhelm us that we were not hovering in separate melancholic spheres, like balloons drifting apart above a parade, but rather, we were joined beneath a banner of Universal Melancholy. It was as if the Creeping De-spair, which hadn't fully succeeded in killing Paul Broth, had come at last to finish the job.

"Soon, by the logic that thought tends inevitably toward ac-tion, a banner was hung by a crew of volunteers. Stretching across the Square, it read: *WE ARE SAD.*

"Summer wore on. June's soothing warmth yielded to July's oppressive heat, and this Universal Melancholy took a more definite form. As we all sat together in the Square, sweltering and trying to gather our thoughts under that banner, we real-ized what it was: the sadness of parting. The awareness that we would all, one day, have to say goodbye. On this day, whenever it came, we would see one another for the last time. Assuming we all died or drifted apart one by one, these partings would be serial, ongoing, inevitable. There could nev-er, it seemed to us in those gruesomely hot July and then Au-gust afternoons, be an end to our Melancholy. There would, much to the contrary, likely come a period when we'd have to part almost daily with someone we loved.

"As we returned home each night to twist and shiver in our sheets, we thought, When will the day come after which I will never see so-and-so again? Has it come already? Was today the day?

"Eventually, the not-knowing grew so profound that a new fixation took hold of us, every bit as forcefully as the Melan-choly had. As summer gave way to autumn, we thought, with no room for negotiation, Let's just leave now."

"Just leave?" I ask, realizing I haven't gotten a word in this whole time. It's scary how overpowering Branson can be. I hadn't, until now, even managed to think in my own voice.

Branson nods, snarling at the interruption. He glances at the gathered fetuses—who are growing restive, their allegiance in question—before looking back at me and continuing his story. "Just leave. We decided that all of us, one day in Septem-ber, would simply walk out of Town and into the Desert, never to meet again. We wrote a Declaration stating as much, and sealed it in a vault in the Records Room of the Town Hall. Packing nothing, we decided to shake hands in Sacrifice Square and then set out. And that'd be it. No more fear of the unknown future moment when this leave-taking would have to occur. We realized we had no power to keep it from happening, but we did have the power to determine its location in time, so we resolved to use that power before it slipped away."

"And you did?" I'm determined to speak more, for fear that otherwise Branson will erase me from the interaction, nullifying any chance I might have to assert myself as the Director of anything. I think about him leaving Town in the story he's telling, and how many times he's done the same thing since. "Sort of your whole M.O.," I want to say, thinking back on his supposed death in 1991, but of course he doesn't let me.

"One morning in September," he continues, "we did exactly what we said we were going to do. We left Town, chanting, 'Goodbye, Goodbye, Goodbye,' as we marched under the *WE ARE SAD* banner, never to gather beneath it again. Just as the Creeping Despair had crept in, we were now creeping out. For a few minutes, we remained visible to one another, but after all walking a mile in our own direction, we reached the point where we were each alone in the Desert. No one was on the same trajectory as anyone else. The worst had come to pass, and here we still were . . . or, I should say, here I still was, since the others were well and truly gone."

He pauses, looking me over, evincing, if I'm not mistaken, relief at finding himself less alone now than he was in the story he's telling. A rare moment of vulnerability, quickly suppressed.

"But that wasn't the end?"

He shakes his head. "It wasn't even the beginning.

●

"I WANDERED in that Desert for what felt like and may well have been ten years," he continues, after making me wait so long I fear his silence may be permanent.

"Eating snakes and tiny ratlike mammals, drinking from cacti and the occasional standing pond, I wandered and thought, bedding down in caves or under the open sky. For the first five years, I thought about what my life had been. I assumed it was going to end in the Desert, so I thought back on what I'd done and seen—basically, nothing. I, like you, had led a wasted life, not even a flash in the pan.

"But then, around year six, the balance shifted. I realized—in what you could call a Moment of Revelation—that I wasn't going to die out there. Not yet. If I'd survived that long, I figured, I was bound to survive longer. Without my having meant for it to, my Life in the Desert had become sustainable. I was still young, I realized; time was still on my side.

"So, for the next five years, I turned my attention to the future. I stopped asking myself, Which hole would you like to die in? and started asking, What would you like to do with all the time you have left? It was a curse and a blessing, as they say, to be vested with a future I hadn't planned on having to account for.

"As the years wore on, I started thinking about Movies. All my memories of my youth and upbringing in Dodge City, and of the great Melancholy that had come over us there, took on a cinematic dimension. I started to think: all of that . . . all of what happened . . . what was it all if not the makings of a Movie?"

He pauses again, staring off into the Desert where we're sitting, which I realize is the same Desert he wandered through all those years ago, coming to the decision that set him on the path whose conclusion he's by now almost reached. All things that seem far away are actually nearby, I think. Everything's superimposed. I open my mouth, but he continues before I work up the courage to say what I've just realized.

"I wandered deeper into the Desert, growing more and more charged with ambition. An ambition I'd previously refused to admit to myself, I now admitted freely, proudly even, feeling it swell in my gut as I shouted at the night sky. 'Nothing can stop me from becoming what I've decided to become, because if anything could, it would have by now!' I shouted.

"Like so, in the spring of 1986, I arrived in a Town. After all those years of sand and dust, I crossed a line out of nowhere and into somewhere. It seemed at once miraculous and inevitable, like I'd simply reached the point I'd been approaching all along. Like I'd conjured this Town through pure force of Will, in my first Conscious Act of Direction, but also that the conjuring was no less predetermined than God's conjuring of the Universe. Indeed, perhaps it was the selfsame event. B.B., as everyone knows, stands both for Blut Branson and Big Bang."

"And the Town you reached was Dodge City?" I force the question out.

Branson smiles, eying me like I'm a precocious five-year-old. "Well, at first I wasn't sure. I walked through a Town that looked familiar, catching the eyes of people who looked familiar, too, though it was hard to tell for sure. I had been so fundamentally altered by my years in the Desert that, even if it was Dodge City, it no longer struck me in the same way. It's like a shell game out there: there are infinite Dodge Cities, but only one of them is real, and you have to be pretty sharp to remember which that is."

"What's the difference?"

"Well, for one thing, the *WE ARE SAD* banner had fallen down. Now, I saw potential where before I'd seen only sadness. All these people, whether they were the old population likewise returned from the Desert, or a new population who'd filled the void we left behind, looked at me with reverence. Awe. All modesty aside, I could feel myself emitting a mythic charge. They knew they were products of my mind, and thus slaves to my Vision. Alive solely to play the roles I cast them in.

"I was the Great Man Returned. Resurrected. These people looked at me like a Messiah, at last incarnated in Flesh rather than merely in Word, grown wise and courageous enough to take my stand. Here He is, they thought, arrived at last to unify us in a waking dream. To make of the Primal Chaos an Ordered Cosmos. To put us to some use, at long last, after so many fallow years. And I thought, Yes, yes. Here I am. Here I am."

"And like so, you took control of Dodge City?"

Branson smiles again. "I didn't have to. I *was* Dodge City, and Dodge City was I. Everything and everyone there lives by the Grace of Me alone."

He doesn't add 'including you,' but I can tell he knows it's what I'm thinking.

"Those people were mine. Absolutely mine. I began work on *The Murder of Nicola Teensmah*—my most personal film, conflating my long years in the Desert with Dan's long years in Prison—that day. With an entire Town's worth of free labor, production went fast. Before long, Branson Entertainments was up and running, an enterprise fully coterminous with The Dodge City Film Industry. Soon we had *Nicola* in the can, playing on the main screen at the Temple, the poster in the Lobby. Then we devoted ourselves to *The Harmless Slaughterer* —also my most personal film, conflating the Slaughterer's mysterious power with my own, the sense in which both he and I could claim knowledge of the Mind of God simply by attaining knowledge of our own minds—and then . . ."

"Then the rest is history," I say, wondering if I'm any more capable of resisting the power of the Great Man than those original stunned Townspeople were. And if I'm not, I wonder what's left. . . . I wonder if maybe I, too, should disappear into the Desert, ready to die there unless fate intercedes. Maybe what worked for him will work for me. Maybe, whether or not he meant to, he returned to teach me this.

Next time I look up, Branson's arranging a shot on the set that I realize is now unambiguously his, and he's far more absorbed in his work than I've ever been in mine.

PHASE VII:
Dr. Gentle

The Gentile Cronenberg

HEAD HUNG, I march into the Desert, leaving Branson to make whatever he will of the set I'd once hoped would serve as the locus of my feature film début. No fetuses follow.

I'm determined to find out if the Desert will absorb me, or if, like Blut, it will eventually deposit me back in Dodge City, or in a new Dodge City, on the far side. Or maybe, I think, as the lights of Branson's set recede, I'll manage to leave this part of the country for good, arriving at last in the Real Los Angeles, with all of America behind me.

I walk in a straight line for what feels like longer than all night, but there's no shift in the dark overhead.

●

TIME TO SLEEP. I find a declivity in the sand and settle into it, staring up at a sliver of moon. As soon as my eyes droop shut, I feel a pair of hands tugging at my sleeve. I keep my eyes closed, hoping the hands will retract if I don't acknowledge them. But this only works in certain stories I've read, and maybe in other parts of the country, in other deserts.

Not here. My sleeve goes on being tugged until I open my eyes.

When I do, I see a mild-looking, gray-haired man wearing a headlamp. It illuminates his features like the text on a page under a flashlight. 'Mild through and through' is my read on him. 'A man either incapable of malice, or one whose malice is so deeply buried it casts no shadow on his surface.' Defenseless as I am, I decide to assume the former.

"Dr. Gentle. Pleased to meet you," he says, extending his hand. I take it, and he tries to pull me up, but I end up pulling him down. I close my eyes against his headlamp's glare and crawl out from under him, get to my feet, then help him to his. When we're both standing, he laughs and adjusts his head-lamp. "Phew," he says.

Then he points the lamp at a donkey, which moans at the dawning awareness that soon it will be freighted with two rid-ers. Dr. Gentle unties its forelegs, which had been hobbled to-gether to keep it from running away, and I climb aboard.

My arms around Dr. Gentle's shoulders, we set out, our Roci-nante wheezing beneath us, one of us Sancho to the other's Quixote.

●

As WE SLOG ONWARD, the sun begins to rise. I have the sus-picion that it isn't cresting the horizon on its way toward over-taking the sky, but rather that we're approaching a country where it's always day, while leaving one where it's always night. I decide to keep this suspicion to myself. "So, Dr. Gen-tle," I say, "what exactly's your deal?"

"Well," he begins, turning on the donkey to face me, "people around here call me the Gentile Cronenberg."

Around where? I wonder. But I just raise my eyebrows, en-couraging him to go on.

"As you likely know," he goes on, "all souls are divided be-tween Jewish and Gentile aspects. As with a wishbone, only one side can predominate, though both continue to exist."

"And the other?"

His face slackens. "The other, well, enters a sort of under-expressed limbo. A half-life, you might say. A living byprod-uct of the process by which a soul becomes what it is. A fetus that stopped developing but lived on."

"As another person?"

Dr. Gentle nods. "Correct. A new person is born, sometimes

in adulthood, once the Jew/Gentile battle, within a given soul, has reached its conclusion."

"So, in your case . . ."

"In my case, the battle was won, in no uncertain terms, by the illustrious Jewish filmmaker David Cronenberg. I, well . . . I'm what's left. The runoff. The Gentile Remnant. A small-sized person, and I don't mind saying it, though I've grown slightly more powerful since Cronenberg's tragic Career Suicide and the FEMA scandals surrounding it. I was born in my mid-thirties as an amateur cameraman and rural cinema studies professor. As a means of giving back in the only way I can, I've pledged my sabbaticals to shepherding lost souls across this vast Desert. My donkey and I lend a helping hand in our own modest way."

He sighs and checks me for understanding, which I feign.

"I content myself with the knowledge that I am not as badly off as the Jewish David Lynch. Now there is truly a man with nothing to live for."

I nod, feeling my feigned understanding harden into something real, unless it's just the look on my face that's hardening. "Are we almost there?" I ask.

"Where?" Dr. Gentle looks at me with extremely concerned eyes.

I shrug. "I'd assumed there was someplace we were going."

He turns back and grips the donkey's reins with a sigh. "They always do."

The Monoliths

NOW THAT OUR ROLES HAVE BEEN provisionally defined, our wandering enters a mellower phase. We're not talking anymore, nor logging the distance to or away from anywhere special. We're beyond hunger and thirst, or at least beyond acknowledging them. Perhaps we're dead, though if we are, it's not as different from being alive as I'd always hoped it would be.

There's nothing to remark on until we pass a field of black Monoliths, so high they make the flat sand feel like the depths of a canyon. Something about how they lean and tip together, full of gaping holes and hanging vines, makes me picture Towers of Babel that toppled from entropy and neglect rather than from Divine Wrath, outtakes from what ultimately became the slim catalogue of Dürer's Masterpieces.

"Don't you mean Bruegel?" Dr. Gentle asks.

I nod before remembering to feign surprise at learning that he can read my thoughts. This deep in the Desert, I think, there's no predicting what might or might not be the case. I wonder how it could've taken this long to find out, then daydream through his answer.

When he's done, we both clear our throats and begin circling the Monoliths, checking them out from all sides.

THOUGH I DON'T MENTION IT to Dr. Gentle—why bother?— they remind me of the M-Tower in Kazakhstan. This, as so much later in life turns out to be, is a version of that. The Monoliths, the M-Tower . . . double M's, I think, to match Blut Branson's double B's.

The Monoliths exude a stale basement reek as well as a dizzying static buzz, like Movies are playing deep in their cores.

Like an Unholy Family unto themselves, I think, unknown, anonymous Movies reproducing in total isolation.

"Think of the Desert as the outer reaches of Amazon Prime," Dr. Gentle says. "Most people picture Amazon Prime as a jungle, a dense, super-fertile continent, but, at its outer edges, it looks like this. These are the digital wastelands where thousands, even millions, of Movies sit, available to stream but entirely unknown. Unloved, unnamed. Unwatched."

He falls silent, waiting for me to respond. I'm not sure how to, so I don't.

"Can I go on?" he asks.

I feel myself falling into a reverie in which these unwatched Movies are those I never made, all the ideas that festered and then turned ghostly in my head, the pages and pages of notes for scripts I've never written, so desperate to attain material form that they've clustered all the way out here.

"It's enough to make a person cry," Dr. Gentle goes on. "To think that all these Movies continue to exist, in a manner of speaking, rather than simply vanishing because no one watches them. Think about it: some of them, most even, have never been seen. Not even by their casts and crew, in some cases, not in their final versions, anyway. Totally abandoned projects, inklings that faded to nothing, moments of insight and whimsy that soured upon touching the screen."

●

I CAN STILL HEAR Dr. Gentle's voice in the background, but it's fading as the voices of the Monoliths grow louder. I hear them whispering, "No! Get out while you still can!" "What's that, some kind of a—?" "He's in there, hiding behind the chifforobe!" "Who, the Mayor? You can't be serious?!" And thousands of other lines, all at once, all in unknown voices, snippets out of context, leading toward no denouement.

I'll watch you, I catch myself thinking. Just slow down, start from the beginning, and let me get my bearings. I'll watch you and never leave; I'll spend my life here watching; I'll be your one Watcher, the one mind between you and oblivion, the only one to hear the tree fall in the forest. That'll be my calling, my . . .

A pair of surprisingly strong hands grabs my shoulders and hoists me to my feet, which leave deep trails in the sand as I'm dragged away. "Close your eyes," I hear Dr. Gentle hiss as he works two gobs of wax into my ears. "They're Sirens. Don't let them suck you in. If you do, you'll never make it out alive."

The Real Blut Branson

WHEN I OPEN MY EYES, I'm high above the Desert, watching the sunset. So much for the notion that we've entered the land where it's always day. I see Dr. Gentle and our donkey on the sand below, sitting quietly, perhaps waiting for me to come down. I'm in no hurry.

I'm back in my M-Tower, I think, as I feel a surge of directorial potency flare up in my core. I'm determined not to waste it. Pacing the stone floors of the Monolith—did the Siren Call tear me away from Dr. Gentle, or did he deposit me here as an inoculation against it?—I sink into a vision of my next Movie, a searing masterpiece that all of Dodge City will be powerless not to worship. It will, I think, as I pull the wax from my ears, be my symbolic execution of Blut Branson, the moment in which I finally step into his shoes and assume the mantle I've so long considered my private birthright. In short, it'll be the Movie where Branson dies at the end, the Crypt finally able to contain him for good.

Remembering that Dr. Gentle can read my thoughts, I invite him in, so that I'm now both directing the Movie and screening it for him, my trusty Assistant Director.

●

THE MOVIE, entitled *The Real Blut Branson*, opens when Blut is diagnosed with a terminal illness and retreats to a hospice set up in his Boyhood Home, on the northern edge of Dodge City. It's a humble, two-story house on a quiet backstreet, a far cry from the later excesses of Branson Mansion. Here, he decides it's time to reveal the full truth about himself, the three percent that he's so far left out of his harrowingly autobiographical filmography. For his final film, he'll direct an entirely unfabricated autobiopic, shot on grainy digital video in the most straightforward possible style, a *style-without-style*, revealing the agony of his early years, his fraught, ambivalent relationship with his father and even more ambivalent reaction to fame, and the subsequent cycle of reclusion and re-emergence that he never managed to break. Until now.

But first, he must choose who will play him in this film-within-the-film, as he's far too sick to both direct and play himself at the same time, though as a younger man there can be no doubt that he would have.

Luckily, Dodge City is full of Blut Impersonators. Indeed, his influence is so pervasive that every citizen is an Impersonator to one degree or another, many of them unwittingly. Though the Impersonators and all their apocryphal films are ritually purged every year, their legions, nevertheless, continue to swell. They keep coming back, whether through a logic of conversion, turning otherwise self-possessed Dodge City citizens into versions of Blut, or reproduction, copying themselves in secret, perhaps deep in The Dodge City Annex, if one believes the version put forth by *Unholy Family*. What's clear is that it's a seasonal, tidal phenomenon in Dodge City. With enough time, the vast majority of Townspeople will end up claiming to be Blut Branson.

Some would even go so far as to claim that all aspects of Dodge City life—going to school, going to work, going shopping, coming home—are, in their own ways, forms of Branson Impersonation, if by 'Impersonation' one also means 'Worship.' Even those involved with the annual Purge of the Impersonators have their own Impersonators, so that one can never be sure whether one's witnessing the actual Ritual or one of its innumerable reenactments. The people of Dodge City are, in this sense, more a fungal than a vegetal race, living as they do always in Branson's fertile dark.

●

I LOOK OFF the edge of the Monolith here to check if Dr. Gentle's listening. His back is to me, leaning against the sleeping donkey, but I trust he's synced up inside. It feels good, I must admit, finally to have an audience.

I cough to expel the static that the Monolith is trying to fill my head with—it is, after all, a Movie of its own, and so would surely prefer I listen rather than think—and continue directing *The Real Blut Branson* as best I can.

It falls to Blut to select an official Impersonator to vest with his legacy since the biopic he's making will end with this Impersonator accepting the lifelong burden of being 'the Real Blut Branson,' taking a solemn oath to continue the Master's career so as, in essence, to deny that the Old Blut ever died. This, of course, may have already occurred more than once in the course of history, but never before has it been explicitly thematized on film.

The early scenes detail the process by which Blut searches for his Impersonator amidst a horde of applicants, directing each one in a few sample episodes from his life—"First Kiss," "Going Away to Film School at Dodge City U," "First Day on the Set of *The Pale Oaks*," "Attempting to Cast an Impersonator to Play Me in *The Real Blut Branson*"—so as to determine the best vessel to live on through.

●

BUT HE FINDS that those Impersonators who most clearly bear the traits that make him who he is—self-pity, melancholia, past-hauntedness, luridness, grandiosity, sleaze—are so distasteful, when viewed in the harsh light of the audition room (the kitchen of his Boyhood Home/hospice), that he can't bear to cast any of them.

At just this moment, a swarthy Hungarian prince, played by a younger version of the star of *The Harmless Slaughterer*, or perhaps that actor's son, bursts onto the scene.

Blut is immediately moved by this Impersonator's Grace, his unthinking self-confidence, his seeming immunity to introspection and looping neurosis. Most of all, he's moved by the Impersonator's seeming imperviousness, even obliviousness, to the audition process. This Impersonator barely seems to know that he's here with hopes of being cast in a film, let alone one revealing the Real Blut Branson once and for all.

The audition lasts fewer than five minutes. Despite the total lack of resemblance and the disapproval of his producers, Blut chooses this last Impersonator in a fit of whimsy the hospice nurses wouldn't have imagined he had left in him.

●

"I SENSE there's more," Dr. Gentle whispers inside my head. I run back to the edge of the Monolith and look out, but the Gentile Cronenberg is still sitting against the donkey, gazing pacifically at the Desert.

"You're right," I think, turning back into the depths of the Monolith. "There sure is."

Things take a new turn. No longer will Blut close the three-percent window of mystery on his life before dying. Rather, his plan is now to open it further. To die with, ideally, one hundred-percent mystery about his True Nature—stretched as it will be between the Blut whom people think they know and the Blut Impersonator they will see onscreen—firmly in place. The people of Dodge City will never know for sure what kind of soul, if any, their idol and guiding light really had. There will be untold future generations of Talmudic scrutiny and internecine strife attempting to parse this very question, which will, naturally, succeed only in obscuring it further.

From here, the Movie details the process by which Blut prepares to hand over his legacy to his successor, high on the fantasy of being transformed into a totally other type of man, one far less hobbled by doubt, while also regretting that the conditions that have made his Art possible will cease to obtain if he undergoes this transformation: the actual fount of his Genius will run dry if he entrusts its safekeeping to this handsome cipher.

All this time, his illness is progressing, clouding his judgment and further blurring the already-blurry boundaries between past and present. He doubles down inside his Boyhood Home /hospice, determined to direct the autobiopic and then die without ever going outside again. He's even designed a burial plot for himself deep in his winter coat closet, beside the grave of his beloved pug, Sparky.

So, directing from his Boyhood Bed, he retells his life as if he'd been the Hungarian prince all along. He films scenes from every stage of his childhood, adolescence, and young manhood, all within this same house, or on sets built to resemble other houses while still being situated within this one.

In his last days, he enters a kind of third-person trance, in which he believes he's watching himself from a disembodied outside perspective. The illness makes his whole body numb, so he can't feel anything except what he imagines his Impersonator must feel.

He is thus entering an undead state, watching himself return to the prime of his life in the body of a much younger man....

●

I BEGIN to waver here, losing track of the story, watching the Hungarian prince gain strength and confidence as he merges with Branson in his Boyhood Bed, until the Movie shifts, seamlessly, into telling the story of Branson's upbringing, in this exact same house, except he's no longer sick, he's no longer dying. . . . He's getting stronger with every scene, preparing to march into the Desert and shut down the very Movie I imagine I'm making right now.

I have a flashback to my seat in the Temple as I realize here that every Monolith has a Temple within it, a private Screening Room where it can present itself as the Marquee Event.

The houselights go dark, and I huddle against the stone walls, listening to the Movie whisper. "The Real Blut Branson . . ." it whispers, and no matter how hard I try to stuff the wax back in my ears, I can't stop it. "The Real Blut Branson is bigger than you. He's stronger and smarter and more powerful, and he goes on forever. All these Movies, even all the way out here in the Desert, are his. Just like your so-called M-Tower. Any film you imagine, any story you try to tell, he will rise from within it to overtake you. These Towers are his surplus, his runoff, the rotting bounty of his Genius, so far beyond you that it's . . ."

I shriek as loudly as I can in a pathetic attempt to drown out the sound. I shriek and shriek until Dr. Gentle appears before me, on the upper landing, astride the donkey. "Think it's time to go?" he asks, his voice calm and earnest.

Swallowing the next shriek I was about to expel, I nod and hold out my arms, letting him hoist me onto the donkey and lead us both down the jagged, winding stairs.

My final thought before blacking out again is, Could it be that Dr. Gentle is an agent of Branson's, sent all the way across the Desert to drag me back to my Room like the disobedient child I've perhaps always been? Was he never anything but a proxy, determined, as they all are, to make sure that no films but Branson's ever get made?

Or, on the contrary, is he my last hope, my lone supporter, the only Assistant Director I'll ever have? The uncertainty rips through my belly, leaving me with the sense that the Schisms that have long divided Dodge City are dividing me, too, as if the longstanding conflation of Blut with the Town has migrated to my body, leaving me as both person and place in one unstable package, bouncing queasily on the back of a donkey.

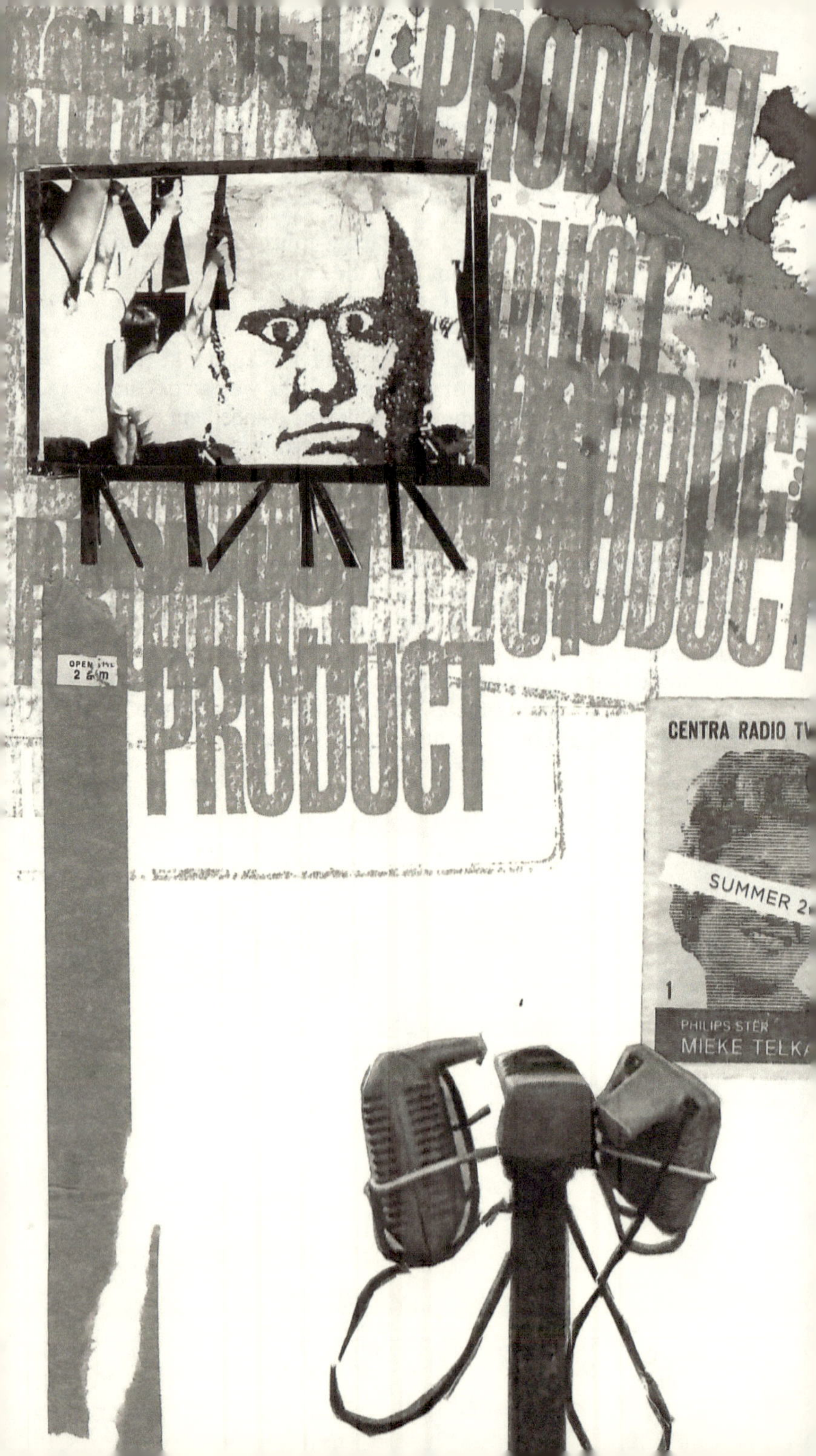
PRODUCT
PRODUCT
PRODUCT
CENTRA RADIO T
SUMMER 2
1
PHILIPS STER
MIEKE TELK

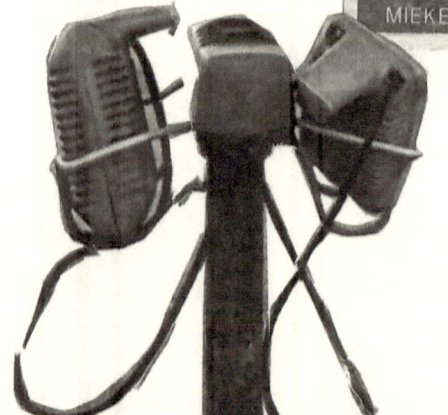

PHASE VIII:

The Dodge City

Film Festival

Back to Town

AFTER DAYS OF BLEARY TRAVEL, a distant skyline comes into focus. As we keep our pace, it only grows clearer. The skyline resolves, predictably, into that of Dodge City, and soon enough we're approaching the Outskirts—Don and Sancho returning from our knightly exploits.

At the edge of the Outskirts, we shed these guises, let our donkey go, and trudge on past the Dead Mall, past the gas station where Drifter Jim presumably still works, and down the same streets I must have trudged up in order to leave Dodge City behind, however long ago that was. All I remember is parting ways beneath the *WE ARE SAD* banner, sometime in the 70s, when *Rabid* was all the rage.

Almost no one's around, and the few people who are seem lost, feebly killing time. Once we've made it through the Outskirts and into Sacrifice Square, it feels like gravity has gone slack, the air pressure so low the buildings are deflating.

"We came to the wrong place?" Dr. Gentle asks, reading my unease, though now I can't trust his apparent innocence. No one's free of Branson's direction, I think, least of all those who seem to be.

"No, no. We're here. It's just . . ." I trail off, uncertain how best to explain what Dodge City was, as opposed to what it now appears to be. The notion seems ephemeral. Maybe everything's fine, or at least no worse than before. Maybe Dodge City was never a stable entity. Maybe it just took on a certain settledness in my mind, during the lonely months away.

●

"LET'S TAKE A SEAT by the fountain and think," I say. As Dr. Gentle and I take our seats by the fountain, a mass of people wanders past us, glum and silent, dragging their heels and hugging their sides.

Discomfited, I snap at Dr. Gentle, "Get us coffee!" It feels good to treat him as my assistant.

He stands, looks around, then runs through the procession, in what I assume he hopes is the direction of a coffee shop.

While he's gone, I sit by the fountain and remember the time —at some point in what I'll now simply call *the past*—when the water crackled with the molten celluloid of Ghost Porn after I'd returned from meeting the Boy Sparklehorse in the Desert. I was young then, I think, squirming where I sit.

●

DR. GENTLE RETURNS with two coffees and a grease-spotted white bag, from which he removes a scone and hands me half.

"You didn't get two?"

His jaw clacks open, and he blushes.

I'm being mean now. I should stop.

"In the coffee shop over there," he begins, tentatively.

I nod for him to continue, chewing my half scone.

"In the coffee shop over there, I heard some folks talking about a film festival. 'The Dodge City Film Festival,' I heard them say."

The Dodge City Film Festival. I've heard Big Pharmakos mention it in the context of The Dodge City Golden Age, but never as a real event, present in real time. During my years here, it's only ever been the Purge of the Impersonators and the Blut Branson Retrospective, in endless alternation.

"Are you certain?"

He nods. "They said it kicks off at dusk. Everyone's gathering at the Drive-In."

"The Drive-In?" This, too, would seem to belong to The Dodge City Golden Age, a relic of an era before the Temple was the only theater in Town, itself waging a losing battle against TV's ubiquity. I've always pictured the Drive-In as a blank screen in a weedy field on the edge of Branson Entertainments.

"Should I get tickets?" Dr. Gentle asks.

I look up, realizing I've burned my eyes on the sunset, scanning it for signs of the Golden Age. I squint, and the atmosphere around me feels soft and warm, like partly melted wax, a mold of a place I'm now receding into. If, in this version of Dodge City, the Film Festival's back on, let's go. "Yeah," I say, "get them now, before they sell out."

The Dodge City Film Festival

Part I: Fellini at the Drive-In

TICKETS IN HAND, Dr. Gentle and I march with what seems like the entirety of The Dodge City Population out to Branson Entertainments.

Concession stands are set up just outside the gate. Barbecues sizzle with racks of ribs and thick salt-crusted steaks, surrounded by beer trucks and cotton candy stations and rows of mobbed porta-potties.

We make our way in, fighting for lawn space between folding chairs and largish encampments of tarps, tents, and trailers. The lights go down in the sense of night falling, and the screen fills with a face I just barely recognize:

Professor Dalton looks older, though his voice is still robust. He is once again clean-shaven, his face tanned around the edges of where his beak mask used to be. "Good people of Dodge City. It is my great pleasure and honor to welcome you all to the first night of The Dodge City Film Festival. It's been a long hiatus since the last one, but as of tonight we are, I'm thrilled to report, back in business. Enjoy the show!"

He vanishes as the screen flickers and crackles and the main event begins.

Fellini's *Amarcord*, that sublime vision of life in Fascist Rimini, with its mix of the sensual and the melancholy, the carnal and the divine and the forty-two-year-old man-child in the tree, throwing stones at his family while screaming, "I want a woman!"

●

I'M SO ENTRANCED it takes a while to notice when it's over and Professor Dalton's face is back onscreen. At first, I conflate him with the film's lascivious but charming elderly narrator and find myself wondering how Fellini knew Dalton.

"It is my great hope that you all enjoyed the film. It is, without a doubt, my all-time favorite specimen of the outside world. To paraphrase the immortal words of the dearly departed Roger Ebert, it is a film filled with images that are 'so inexplicable and irreproducible that all the heart can do is ache with gratitude,' leaving the viewer with the feeling that 'he will live forever, love all the women, drink all the wine, make all the movies, and become Fellini.'"

Dalton takes a moment to dry his eyes with a baby-blue handkerchief before continuing. "However, you are assembled here tonight for a purpose beyond that of entertainment, however sublime said entertainment may inarguably be. As you are all aware, a Foundation Crisis has occurred in the order of The Dodge City Film Industry."

This is the last thing we want to hear, vulnerable as we all still are to the effects of what we've just seen. Probably the exact reason Dalton chose to tell us now, I think, my respect for him returning.

"Blut Branson, longtime scion of our Film Industry and closest thing to a Culture-Hero this Town has ever had, is gone." Dalton's face is nearly popping off the screen now, tears streaming down his cheeks. "Dead, disappeared, abdicated . . . who can say? All we know for sure is that he is, by this point, unlikely to return, despite the many resurgences he's made in the past. This time, I must say, feels different.

"So, steps must be taken. The Dodge City Film Festival is a joyous occasion, but it is not only that. This year, it must be more. Much more. It is to be a competition. A vetting of visionaries. A test to see who among you, with ample funding and resources, can produce a film that convincingly mythologizes our origins here in Dodge City, as Fellini has done to such an overwhelming degree for his origins in Fascist Rimini."

I hear bodies shifting in the badly mowed grass, some kissing like teenagers, others scooting closer to the screen.

"Whoever produces the most effective filmed testament to life as it was during The Dodge City Golden Age will be crowned the New Branson, and elected Culture-Hero for life. He or she will be put in full control of Branson Entertainments, and the full attention of Dodge City, including its Annex and inexhaustible supply of Assistant Directors, will be upon him or her forever. Our folk religion will reorient itself around you. A new Golden Age will begin."

He stops to clear his throat, as do I. It's a lot to process.

"You will all receive a duffel bag full of cash for production expenses on your way out. Furthermore, The Dodge City Schoolchildren will be at your full disposal, should you wish to recreate scenes from your childhood using them."

Here he pauses to gesture from the screen at a bullpen full of children in the grass behind us. We turn to regard them, smashed together like asylum seekers at a ferry launch in Tripoli. "They'll be penned up at the school, free for the taking. First-come, first-served.

"It's a tall order, but, at this point, the void in our spirit-life must be filled. May the Best Director win! I will see you all back here for the final screening one month from tonight." With that, his image boils away, and the Drive-In screen goes black.

●

WE ALL SIT THERE, stunned in the cricket and mosquito buzz, until the real Dalton, microscopic compared to his filmed counterpart, shouts, "All right, folks!"

I look over and see him standing at the entrance gate, flanked by bodyguards.

Dr. Gentle gets to his feet and takes my hand, helping me up, successfully this time. When we pass the entrance, Dalton holds open a duffel bag, showing us the cash inside before zipping it up and handing it over.

"Spend it wisely," he warns.

I Direct My Amarcord

THE NEXT ORDER OF BUSINESS IS TO CHECK back into the Hotel. It's strangely emotional, approaching the Front Desk and asking for my old Room, like the very first time I drifted into Dodge City.

"Do you mind waiting over there by the fish tank?" I ask Dr. Gentle, feeling myself tear up as I revisit that long-ago morning.

"He's gonna have to pay, too," says the Concierge. "It's too late to sneak him in."

I nod. "That's not the problem," I say, showing her the duffel bag full of cash. "I just . . ."

She seems to understand. The rest of the transaction goes smoothly, and soon, just like my very first day in Dodge City, the Porter has shown me to my Room.

●

WHEN WE'VE SETTLED IN, Dr. Gentle in a child-sized cot the Porter wheeled out of storage for him, and me in my old bed, we pour ourselves mezcals from the minibar and get down to business.

"Okay," says Dr. Gentle, pen and legal pad open on his lap. "Got any ideas?"

WE SPENT the first week of our allotted production month spitballing in my Room. *The Real Blut Branson*, though it's still foremost in my mind, feels too heady for this context, unlikely to win over a Drive-In audience on a first viewing.

"It could be a . . ."

"No," I'd say.

"What about a . . ."

"No," I'd say.

"Oh, I know . . . what if we had these two . . ."

"No," I'd say, growing frustrated with him, and by extension myself, since I'd so far failed to come up with anything better.

Room Service trays piled up around us, and my bill from the minibar became one more thing I was refusing to think about. Every day around four, Dr. Gentle would ask if he could go to the Health Center to blow off steam, and I'd say, "No," then regret it, then a few minutes later say, "Okay, fine."

I'd watch reruns of *Unholy Family* while he was gone, one eye on the duffel bag, half-expecting the cash to go off after so long unused. I could picture it climbing up the wall and onto the windowsill, sliming the glass open, and crawling down the side of the building.

Then Dr. Gentle would come back, sweating and happy, and ask, "What did I miss?" and I'd point to the TV screen.

●

THIS FALLOW PERIOD COMES to a forced end when Dalton calls on the Room's landline and says, "The Schoolchildren are getting picked over. If you want any, I'd suggest you get yourself to the school today."

Though I'd just worked up the energy to go to the Health Center, I nod to Dr. Gentle. "Get our cash. Let's go."

●

WHEN WE ARRIVE AT THE SCHOOL, we push our way inside, following the paper signs on the wall that read CASTING with arrows pointing first to the left and then, after rounding a corner, to the right.

We come down a half-flight of stairs into a cavern with a more permanent sign outside that reads ART ROOM in English and braille. Posters of waterlilies, haystacks, and Picasso, shirtless and feral in his studio, adorn the walls.

No one's around, not even Dalton, whom I'd somehow expected to see here. No one but six glum children sitting on carpet squares inside a wire enclosure, surrounded by wrappers and crumbs. The ceiling fan drifts in slow circles; the lighting's a dreary afternoon yellow.

They barely look up as we enter. "So, which one's you?" Dr. Gentle asks, after we've seen them from every angle.

I stop short, clear my throat. "What?"

Dr. Gentle shrugs and gives one of his self-deprecating smiles. "Nothing . . . I just meant, er, don't you want to cast one of them as you and the others as your friends, so the Movie can be about your years growing up in Dodge City?"

I can't tell if Dr. Gentle actually thinks I'm from here, or if he's just having this idea now, but it's the smartest thing either of us has said since this whole process began. It only seems obvious because it should have been. It is, I think, a quintessentially Gentile idea. No Jew would ever dream of being *from* somewhere. Our story is always that of exile, even in the places we were exiled from.

"Oh, right. That's what I meant," I say, though I know he can tell it isn't. "That's exactly what I had in mind."

Dr. Gentle shrugs again, seemingly happy for me to take credit. "How about this one? Were you a fat kid?" He points to a fat kid in goldenrod corduroys and a purple T-shirt with a dinosaur egg hatching out of its front pocket.

Was I a fat kid? I can barely remember. Then I squeeze my belly and think, Yes. Yes, I guess I was. I must've been. That must've been the defining trauma that gave rise to my Genius.

"Okay, you." I point at the fat kid. He doesn't respond until I walk directly into his line of sight and snap my fingers. Then he yawns and leaves his mouth open.

"What?" he finally says, his voice high and phlegmy.

"You, you're cast. You're gonna be in a Movie! Isn't that great?"

He yawns again and picks his nose. I feel myself losing my cool and decide to leave the area before I lash out. "Bag him up, Dr. Gentle."

"What?" Dr. Gentle asks, pulling me back from the precipice of mania.

"I mean, here, give him this, and tell him he's hired." I pull five twenties from the duffel bag and hand them over.

It's exciting to feel anger rise in me, approaching the edges of my body without spilling over. As if I were capable of the kind of hyper-masculine rage I've seen Blut Branson fly into. As if, all along, that had been latent somewhere within me.

I wait by the rotten-smelling milk cooler, trying to remember my own school days, wherever they were, whatever the school looked like then. Did I have art class? Did I drink the milk, back when it was still good?

●

WE RETURN to the Hotel and install the fat kid and three others in the Health Center, abandoned except for a custodian refilling the water cooler, who hurries away when he sees us.

"So," Dr. Gentle says, hoisting the duffel bag with our cash onto his shoulder, appointing himself its de facto guardian. "Let's start blocking out scenes."

I try to think back on what in *Amarcord* moved me most. The deranged man in the tree, the peacock in the snow, the Grand Hotel that the Townspeople are never allowed to enter . . .

"Okay," I tell the fat kid. "Let's rehearse a scene where you're in your room, dreading another summer alone with your Primal Father, with whom you live in mutual enmity, when you hear that your cousins will be visiting from California."

Whatever toll it takes on these kids, I think, trying to make my voice sound like Branson's in my head, I'm going to direct a convincing version of a Dodge City Childhood and claim it as my own. No longer will I be from nowhere, a Drifter in a rented Room, biding his time. No, from now on, if I finish what I'm here setting out to do, the fact that I grew up in Dodge City will be undeniable, a matter of public record. I'll be the native son made good, the groundwaters of this Town at last flowing to the surface through me.

●

"LET'S FIND some creek beds," I say after our third day of rehearsals, mustering Dr. Gentle and the cast out of the Health Center and into the parking lot behind the Hotel. "Some cornfields. A candy store. A comics store. The old train station where I used to sit on lazy Saturday afternoons and wait for the Silver Bullet to roll through. The rack where I used to wait salivating for the new month's dime novels to be unloaded off the truck. The ones I read in a day and stuffed under my bed, where they swelled into a monstrous mass of damp, colorful paper, whispering to me at night to supplement my dreams. All the halcyon signifiers of a ruddy American childhood, deep in The Dodge City Golden Age, gathered here at last, all in one place, projected across the Drive-In screen for all to see."

I catch my breath, expecting something to happen. When nothing does, I clear my throat. "I'll scout locations with the kids," I say. "You go to DCTV, and get the equipment. We'll meet at the fairgrounds at seven."

Dr. Gentle nods, and we depart, the fat kid who'll play me followed by three others—two girls and a boy, who will play my cousin, Anne; my cousin, Denny; and my best friend, Corinne—all names and roles I've made up on the spot.

●

OVER THE NEXT TWO WEEKS, we film the canonical scenes, all set during the summer when my cousins and my best friend and I were between nine and thirteen, and we had the experiences that made us who we then became. In my case, this meant creeping out of the shadow of my Primal Father and into the loose but authentic skin of my future self, a sentient, autonomous being at large in an entropic universe.

The Rubicon Summer, after which none of us would be the same. After which Death became real to us, and the Creeping Despair finally found where we'd been hiding, just as surely as it found Paul Broth and, perhaps, Blut Branson.

With Dr. Gentle behind the camera and managing sound, I direct the kids in poignant scenes of loss and discovery. They see their first dead body, crushed under a trailer at the back of the fairgrounds; their first conjoined couple, on a bench we drag to the center of an otherwise abandoned clearing in the woods to one side of the park behind the Dead Mall; they try alcohol in the lot next to Giant Chinese, sipping at a half-empty bottle of Jim Beam we plant in a trashcan for them to discover; they discuss ghosts and eternal life while lying under the stars by the edge of the dry canal that runs through the center of Town; they meet a wildman with a permanent erection and glowing red eyes scuttling from rooftop to rooftop in the most trailer-trash part of the Annex; they find a suitcase full of money—all the twenties from our production budget wrapped around stacks of ones—in the burned-out hulk of a Volkswagen and have to decide what to do, devolving into mutually deceitful factions when no consensus can be reached; and, finally, they skinny dip together in Meyers Pond, leaping into the air on the count of three to display their nascent genitalia for a split second, concretizing their heretofore fluid notions of sexual difference. The harsh reality of being one thing or the other slams home.

At the end of this summer, they go to The Dodge City Kiddie

Funfair one last time, reprising a scene from early in the shoot. But now, I film them walking past the rides in the early autumn twilight as the clowns and strongmen and trapeze artists in melting makeup break down the tents and pull up the stakes, preparing to say goodbye. The caramel apple vendors pulp their soggy remnants, and all the prizes that nobody won get boxed up for next year. Soon, only the streetwalkers and the cripples and the animals too old and sick to perform will remain in what had been, until now, a site of exuberant transgression, safe and unsafe in perfect harmony.

●

WHEN THE SCHOOL YEAR BEGINS, my cousins will go back to Petaluma while my best friend, Corinne, is moving away with her parents on short notice. Even she barely knows why, or where. "Somewhere up north," she says. "Misconsin, Winnesota . . ."

They'll leave me alone to grow up in Dodge City with only my memories of this one magical, melancholy summer to get me through middle and then high school in the House of my Father, himself a failed Director. Then I'll fight my way into adulthood, through odd jobs and debt and uncertainty, eventually to take up the mantle of filmmaking, first as a fledgling, trying out techniques, searching for my voice amidst the din of my influences . . . until, finally, I become the Greatest Director This Town Has Ever Known, a force of nature fit to take on the legacy of Blut Branson himself, to take up the Name of Blut as if for the first time.

"Okay? Should I turn off the, um . . . I'm turning it off now?" I look up to see Dr. Gentle powering down the camera. Still high on my Branson fantasy, part of me wants to scream at him to keep filming, but I resist. He's done nothing wrong. The film's wrapped. I've made my *Amarcord*, cementing myself into The Dodge City Golden Age. Never again will my vision falter, as it did inside the Monolith.

Are you sure? I think I hear Dr. Gentle ask, telepathically, but I ignore the question. Clearing my throat, I say, "Let's get these kids some Dairy Queen and send them home."

The Dodge City
Film Festival Part II

THE DAY OF THE FILM FESTIVAL ARRIVES. After a frantic weekend of editing in the A/V room at Dodge City High, helped by some old man whose name I never learned but whom I referred to privately as *my beloved first film teacher,* we have a rough cut ready to screen.

Unsurprisingly, it's accepted into the Festival. The surprise is that it's selected to screen first. The Opening Night Gala. Black Tie, Red Carpet.

Dr. Gentle and I rent tuxes from a pop-up dry cleaners in the Dead Mall and get to the Drive-In early, ready to field interviews and pose for pictures, but aside from two *Unholy Family* reporters who ask if we noticed any strange activity among the extras while we were shooting, there's not much going on.

Many of the food and drink vendors from the last time we gathered here are back, or here still. Everyone's milling around, eating meat off dripping paper plates.

Then it's time. Dalton strides through the grass in front of the screen, takes a cordless mic from his suit pocket and says, "All right, folks, here's the moment we've all been waiting for. The time for our collective mythology to be refreshed. The long drought of Branson's absence is over. The dawn of the New Branson is nigh. One filmmaker among us tonight will claim the mantle. Please enjoy."

He turns off the mic, slips it back in his suit pocket, and walks into the grass as my *Amarcord* starts up.

●

FOR THE NEXT HOUR AND A HALF, I'm the closest thing Dodge City has to an American Fellini. My vision matters;

my version of childhood touches the canon and begins to rede-
fine it. The audience members revise their own memories to
better fit the version I'm showing them. This, I think, is why
dictators invariably love Movies.

It's an incredible rush. It's like everything I've worked for all
these years is coming to fruition, like I'm passing through the
narrow gateway between being no one and being someone, a
passage as momentous as being born. I'm so deep inside this
feeling that by the time I hear my name, I have the sense that
Dalton's been calling it for a while.

I snap-to, rolling to my feet when I see that he's motioning me
into the circle of light beneath the screen. When I get there, he
claps me on the back and produces a second mic from his
other suit pocket.

I take it and tap its head to test if it's on. It is.

"Well, that was just extraordinary," he says. "I had no idea
you were from here."

I nod, then say, "Yeah."

"Well, I'm sure the audience has questions. Why don't we cut
right to the chase here and open it up to . . ."

●

As I remember it, this is the exact instant when I look out on
the crowd and see, instead of hundreds of rapt faces, a single
lurking madman in torn jeans and a cowboy shirt. He's like
the raving Lear from Kurosawa's *Ran*, his beard tattered and
white, his eyes full of hate and hellish vision. Branson, back
from the Desert.

"H-h-hi, Blut," I stammer into the mic, just before he grabs it
out of my hand and pushes me back into the screen.

The crowd is riveted on him as he clears his throat and speaks.
"You're all probably wondering where I was. I know it's been
a while. I did time in Dead Sir. I went down in that swamp

and did some thinking. I had to cross the whole Desert in order to dry off. During that time, I came to some conclusions.
I got my strength back."

He pulls off his cowboy shirt and his jeans, and then, naked,
peels back his skin, starting with his face and working his way
down. It comes off like wet paper, piling up by his feet. Beneath, he's thin, strong, young, wearing a sleek tailored suit
and white sneakers. Probably younger than me, I think.

"I saw things down there," he continues, his voice supple and
fresh now. "I got some things straight in my mind." He kicks
the pulp of his old self into the grass. I can smell its porky reek
from where I stand propped against the screen.

"I came to understand that what all of you here, tonight, con-
sider to be the Real Dodge City is nothing but a simulacrum.
A film set at best. A version of someone's memory of Dodge
City that you've all tried to convince yourselves is real. I be-
lieved it once, too, but no more. No! No, I tell you tonight.
This is not the Real Dodge City. This is a Traitor's Dodge
City. An American Babylon." Here he turns to look at me, un-
repressed violence in his eyes.

The Return of the Primal Father, grown superpotent, I think,
remembering my Freud, or my Lacan, whoever it was who
said that way back when, in a book I read once on a bus, or in
a bus station. 'If you knock me down, you better kill me,' says
the Primal Father. 'Because if you don't, I'll come back twice
as strong and three times as angry.'

"No, good people," he goes on. "The Real Dodge City, the
genuine one, the one you all deserve to live in, where life is
still in its Golden Age, is in the Deep Desert. Past Dead Sir,
past the Monoliths, past the horizon itself. Follow me, and I
will lead you there. Follow me now."

He drops the mic and strides back through the grass. As he
goes, the Townspeople—my audience—rise entranced to their
feet and fall in line behind him, their backs to the screen.

Before he joins the procession, Dalton picks up the mic and

stammers, "Blut, please forgive us. We never seriously intended to replace your vision with anyone else's. The very notion,
as any good citizen of Dodge City will tell you, is absurd. We
merely had to do what it took to call you back . . . to ensure
you understood the gravity of our bereavement in your absence . . . the spiritual and aesthetic poverty we'd fallen into,
such that we'd . . . such that . . ." He looks at me here, and I
can tell what he means is that the very notion of accepting my
Amarcord as part of a new canon is a mark of shame he can
only pray Branson will overlook.

"We only did all this in order to summon you," Dalton pleads.
"We were desperate."

I hope he roasts you alive, I think, as I watch Dalton drop the
mic into the grass and run to catch up with the departing
Townspeople, all of them huddled in Branson's shadow. I
watch them go, Dr. Gentle among them. He was only ever in
it for the Desert travel, I think. He was never tied to me in particular.

The kids who played my cousins and me in my *Amarcord* are
in the herd, too, as are Big Pharmakos and Gottfried Benn.
Soon, it's just the pulp of Branson's body and I, leaning
against the empty Drive-In screen.

EPILOGUE 1:

The Director's Chamber

S O, this is my Kingdom, I think, as the last stragglers vanish over the horizon. I have won the Mythic Struggle.

I walk out of the Drive-In field and into the empty lots and warehouses of Branson Entertainments, past the golf carts and the dollies and the crates of audio gear and the pallets of wood marked FOR DEAD MALL SET and FOR BUS STATION SET.

I explore the sound stages, the mixing boards, the recording booths. The intake room where I was interviewed before my mission to Kazakhstan. The lever that released the gas that knocked me out. The means of production are mine. All of this, relinquished, left in my charge. I am now both the Minotaur and the Labyrinth.

●

EMBOLDENED BY THIS THOUGHT, I show myself into the office where Branson made all his directorial decisions, modeled after the glass enclosure where the dwarf-Director in *Mulholland Dr* sits in his wheelchair and commands his goons.

I get in the wheelchair now and lean back, putting my lips to the microphone that wraps around the headrest's edge. I clear my throat and whisper, "Play."

The wall across from me lights up and boils with static. Closing my eyes, I imagine I'm watching a Movie detailing my glorious future here in Dodge City, just as vividly as my *Amarcord* detailed my past.

In this future Movie—entitled, naturally, *The Real Blut Branson* —I am the exalted visionary, and Dodge City is full of my acolytes, all False Bransons abandoned in the Desert, cast off as the charlatans they are and always were. My flock has returned to me, my eminence unquestioned now, beyond usurpation. The ranks of the faithless purged, never to regrow. The Unholy Family disbanded for good.

I nod off. When I wake up, the Movie's over. Yawning and stretching without leaving the wheelchair, I clear my throat and whisper, "Rewind."

EPILOGUE 2:

Return to Branson Mansion Part III

STUMBLING OUT of the Director's Chamber after several more viewings, I decide I can no longer inhabit my old Room at the Hotel. I'm something more now, something better: a big deal in this Town, no longer a nameless Drifter in a rented bed, watching a rented TV. I deserve to live like a king, and I know there's only one place where I can.

Head held high, I climb into the Hollywood Hills and make my way along the clifftop path and into Branson Mansion. I help myself to the remains of a roast in the fridge, no longer worried about how old it might be, and open a bottle of wine.

Settling into an armchair in the library, I put on a Roy Orbison record and begin the slow, delicate task of signing all the copies of *Branson on Branson,* in every language, making them all my own.

When I'm finished, I leave the record playing and go upstairs to take a bath. Then I fall asleep in the massive bed, dreaming of the Movie I'll begin work on tomorrow.

●

A HARSH DAWN WAKES ME UP, and I go downstairs in a white robe to make coffee. As it's brewing, I look out the window, expecting to revel in my view of the Hollywood sign and the distant Pacific.

But something else shines through instead: squinting in the glaring sun, I see the Desert come into focus. When the coffee-maker beeps, I fill my mug and return to the window, sipping as the Monoliths I discovered with Dr. Gentle come fully into view, seeming to rise with the sun, shimmering and black. Then I close my eyes, imagining I'm standing in their shadow, about to make my way in.

EPILOGUE 3:

I Build My M-Tower

at Long Last

I ROAM the abandoned streets of Dodge City, a revenant, a scavenger in what is now nothing but a disused set, a collection of alleys and storefronts built to look like a Town but animated by no spirit.

Or no spirit but my own. Everything I can see, I tell myself, is nothing but whatever I decide it is, which is to say it's nothing but whatever I am.

●

IN THIS FRAME OF MIND, I find myself back in the Desert, astride the donkey I rediscovered in the parking lot behind the Dead Mall. We ride in the direction of the Monoliths, toward the forgotten fringes of Amazon Prime.

I stand in their shadow and gaze at the obscure reaches of their upper floors, and wonder at the vision that went into making them, the passion, the pain of the unknown Directors who melted down their lives only to build a Ghost Town, to offer up that which nobody wanted.

Rather than crying, though I'd like to, I gather Branson's robe more tightly around myself and pry a stone loose from the foundation of the nearest Monolith. Like the slaves conscripted to build the Great Pyramid, the donkey and I drag it back to Dodge City, where I place it in the hole that the Cronenberg effigy used to occupy, in the heart of Sacrifice Square.

●

THE NEXT DAY, we make the journey again, and drag another stone, aware that soon this Monolith, and with it all of the unknown Directors' innermost ideas, will collapse, leaving nothing but a pile of rubble, a crowning vision reverting to raw material, as perhaps all visions, no matter how sublime, eventually must.

We make the journey again and again over the following weeks, toppling first one Monolith and then another and then another, until Amazon Prime resembles a shoddy Stonehenge. I pile all the stones in Sacrifice Square, at first without design—simply letting them fall where they may—but, as time goes on, the nature of what I'm building becomes impossible to deny.

I am, here in the heart of what used to be Dodge City, recreating my M-Tower from the Kazakh Steppe, or perhaps creating it for the first time, if the one I discovered as a Location Scout was merely a premonition.

In here, I think, lies my True Vision, that which will finally distinguish me from Blut Branson, or allow me to become the Blut Branson I've always, in my heart, known I could become, if only I summoned the courage to see the transformation all the way through. The courage to leave my old self—the Drifter who came to Dodge City on a bus, planning to drift on—behind for good.

●

I SET the donkey free and climb inside the Tower, making my way to the topmost floor, unconcerned by the instability of the spiral staircase, since I now feel myself to be immortal. From the very top, I dangle my legs off the edge and look out at the Desert, extending past the rubble of the former Monoliths and all the way to the horizon, and I wonder if my Tower, with me inside it, is already sending a signal, a beacon to weary travelers looking for a Town to shelter in.

I hope it is. Come, I think, in their hypothetical direction. If you're out there, come in, come to Dodge City and populate its streets and abandoned stores. Come, and populate my Movies, be my cast and crew and extras, and together we'll create a new canon, a radically new vision of divinity that, in time, will grow undeniable, strong enough to serve as the bedrock for the rest of our lives, and our children's lives, and our children's children's, a cinematic legacy that will go deeper and spread further than Blut Branson's ever did.

Deeper, I think, than the False Blut Branson's ever did. Because now—I can hear myself shouting, into the hot, sandy evening, hoping the Desert winds will carry my voice and galvanize the faithless wherever they roam—"Now, at long last, the Real Blut Branson is born!"

LOOKING DOWN, I see that my limo has arrived, so I descend the many levels of the edifice I've constructed, truly ready, for the first time in my life, to go to work.

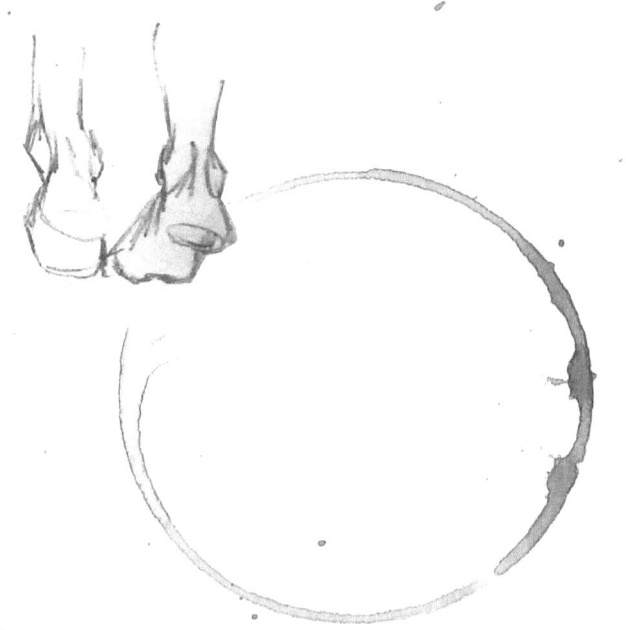

fin

ABOUT *the Author*

DAVID LEO RICE is a writer and animator living in New York City. He's the author of the novels *A Room in Dodge City*, *The PornME Trinity*, and *Angel House*, one of Dennis Cooper's favorite books of 2019. David's debut story collection, *Drifter*, is forthcoming in mid-2021, and his next novel, *The New House*, is forthcoming in 2022. He's online at raviddice.com.

ABOUT *the Artist*

HOSHO MCCREESH is currently writing and painting in the gypsum and caliche badlands of the American Southwest. His work has appeared widely in print, in audio, and online.

AUTHOR *Acknowledgments*

Sincere and heartfelt thanks to Leah Angstman, for her wisdom, vision, and guidance throughout this multiyear project —it wouldn't exist without her. Thanks also to Matthew Spellberg, Michael Natalie, Isaac Shivvers, Andrei Cristea, Kyle Rose, and Eli Epstein-Deutsch for reading and discussing as this volume developed, and to my wife, Ingrid, and my parents, Lynn and Richard, for everything, since the beginning. Further thanks to Kayla Escobedo and Pearse Anderson for running excerpts of this book at *Nat. Brut* and *Weird Fiction Review*. Last but not least, thanks to Hosho McCreesh, for the incredible illustrations, and to Simon Pummell, who taught me what filmmaking is all about.

COLOPHON

The edition you are holding is the First Edition of this publication.

The cover title and interior fonts are set in a combination of Ludovicos, created by SDFonts; Gipsiero Kracxed, created by Bumbayo Font Fabrik; and Essays 1743 Italic, created by John Stracke. The Alternating Current Press logo is set in Portmanteau, created by JLH Fonts. All other fonts are set in Calisto MT. All fonts used with permission; all rights reserved.

Cover artwork by Leah Angstman, with elements by Sofie Layla Thal, Ami at SGND, Maret Hosemann, and Wendy Corniquet. All interior artwork created by Hosho McCreesh, ©2021, hoshomccreesh.com. The Alternating Current lightbulb logo created by Leah Angstman, ©2013, 2021 Alternating Current. Scroll graphic created by Tanya at Clker. David Leo Rice's photo by Sebastian Siadecki, ©2021. Hosho McCreesh's photo by Freddie De La Cruz, ©2021. All images used with permission; all rights reserved.

alternatingcurrentarts.com

www.ingramcontent.com/pod-product-compliance
Lightning Source LLC
Chambersburg PA
CBHW031233260626
47169CB00007B/2274